RHINOCEROS

WARNE'S
WELCOME
BOOKS

THE PLUNDER PIT

WARNE'S WELCOME BOOKS

List of the Titles in this Series

For Boys

By R. Ernest Bailey
THE CLOCK STRIKES TWELVE

By T. C. Bridges
DEAD MAN'S GOLD
THE PLUNDER PIT

By Hylton Cleaver
THE PILOT PREFECT

By Frank W. Howe
KING'S MESSENGER

By T. H. Scott
THE FIGHT FOR THE CUP

For Girls

By Constance Evans
THE BROWN ROSE
THE SECRET RIVER

By Margaret C. Field
THE FRANKLIN MYSTERY

By Mary Gervaise
PENELOPE, PICKLES AND PAM

By Ethel Talbot
BROWNIE ISLAND
SEA RANGERS' HOLIDAY

OF ALL BOOKSELLERS

Published by
FREDERICK WARNE & CO., LTD.
LONDON & NEW YORK

THE FORCE OF HIS RUSH KNOCKED THE FELLOW OFF HIS FEET.
The Plunder Pit. *p.* 57

THE PLUNDER PIT

BY

T. C. BRIDGES

AUTHOR OF
"SONS OF THE AIR," "THE RIVER RIDERS,"
ETC.

FREDERICK WARNE AND CO., LTD.
LONDON AND NEW YORK

Printed in Great Britain
B1-1163

CONTENTS

CHAPTER		PAGE
I.	The Seventh Wave	7
II.	The Black Hole	13
III.	The Big Man	19
IV.	The Rift	24
V.	Torgan Talks of Poachers	30
VI.	Noise in the Night	35
VII.	The Empty Boat	41
VIII.	A Second Search	47
IX.	Down the Vein	52
X.	The Storm Breaks	56
XI.	A Way Out	62
XII.	Danger	66
XIII.	A Sound of Steps	71
XIV.	The Chimney	75
XV.	Chad's Close Call	80
XVI.	Wanda's Warning	85
XVII.	Enemy's Work	90
XVIII.	Chad's Bad Dream	94
XIX.	Jan Loses Heart	99

CONTENTS

CHAPTER		PAGE
XX.	Wanda Wakes	103
XXI.	Voices from the Pit	108
XXII.	Chad, the Scapegoat	112
XXIII.	The Third Man	118
XXIV.	Tidying Up	123

THE PLUNDER PIT

CHAPTER I

THE SEVENTH WAVE

THUD—wump ! The sound was like the firing of a great gun, and the echoes came booming slowly and majestically across the flat surface of the sea to hammer back from the tall limestone cliffs of North Devon. Clive Medland, lying flat in the stern of the small boat, jumped up in a hurry and looked towards the north-west whence the sound had come.

"Thunder, Chad," he said sharply.

"Couldn't be anything else," agreed Chadwyck in his deep quiet voice, and he began to pull in his heavily-weighted fishing line. "You might get up the anchor, Clive."

There was no need for the request, for Clive was already in the bow, hauling in coils of dripping rope. Anything that wanted doing, Clive did in a hurry. The small anchor came clanking in and the thunder rolled again, louder than before. Out to sea a black cloud was rising. It was tipped with rolls of white like fluffs of cotton wool, and already the glass-smooth surface of the long swells were rippled by the first breath of wind.

Chad glanced at the coming storm, and his grey eyes narrowed slightly. Then his big body came to sudden life, he seized a rope, the sail shot up, he made the rope fast to a cleat, shifted swiftly into the stern and seized his tiller. The sail filled and the boat, lying over, began to hiss through the water.

White fire lit the heart of the cloud, and thunder bellowed again. Clive frowned as he stared at the swiftly approaching tempest, and noted the direction of the wind.

"We'll never make it back to Bulport," he said.

"We're not trying it," Chad said briefly, and pointed to a narrow opening in the cliffs almost dead ahead. "We'll run in there and shelter till it's over."

"Good notion," Clive agreed. "What cove is that?"

"The mouth of the Badger Brook. That's all I know, for I've never been in there. But there's shelter and that's all that matters." A gust struck the boat as he spoke and heeled her until the foam seethed along her gunwale. Chad let out the sheet; she righted and sped on towards the coast.

Every minute the wind increased, then the great cloud swept over the sun and instantly everything was plunged in deep shadow, lit every few moments by the blaze of lightning.

"Lucky for us there's a harbour handy," Clive said, picking up a baler. "The dinghy wouldn't last long in this." He was right, for already wave tops were breaking over the small boat and he had to bale hard to keep her from filling.

Chad nodded, and held the boat straight for the gap opposite. Already waves were leaping in white spouts against the tall cliffs on either side of the opening. Their roar grew louder every minute and the crashes of thunder more frequent. Suddenly Clive gave a shout.

"Look, Chad! Look."

He pointed to the cliff foot at the right of the gap, where a slim figure clung to a ledge just above the wave tops. Chad looked.

"A girl!" he cried, and without a moment's hesitation swung the boat round towards her. Clive held his breath. He didn't see a hope either for them or the girl. Once in the grip of those breakers, the boat would be lifted and smashed to matchwood on the iron-hard rocks. But Chad showed no sign of nervousness.

"Drop the sail, Clive. Take the boat-hook. Fend off, if you can," he ordered. Clive let the sail down with a run and grabbed the boat-hook. Chad shipped the oars and used all his great strength to hold the dinghy off the rocks.

"Jump!" Clive yelled to the girl.

She had already turned and was standing with her back to the cliff. She was rather white, yet although the waves were breaking over her knees, Clive saw that she was quite cool.

She was gathering herself to jump when the big wave came. Two men could not have held the boat against it. The light craft was raised on its crest and flung with a crash against the cliff. Quite what happened in the next few seconds Clive hardly knew, but when the wave had dropped back, he found himself on the ledge next the girl and Chad on the other side of him. Some planks and two oars were floating beneath them, all that remained of the dinghy.

"Hold on!" cried the girl. "Another wave coming." Long trails of seaweed hung from the ledge above. She twisted her fingers among them and the boys did the same. The next wave washed to their waists, but they hung on. As it sank back the girl spoke to Clive.

"There's another ledge above. If I got on your shoulders I could do it."

"All right. Be quick," Clive snapped, and up she went light and nimble as a squirrel. Clive felt her jump, then she was off his shoulders and lying flat on the ledge above.

"Come on," she called. "I can help you now."

Clive waited for the next wave to come and fall, then made a frantic scramble and, with the girl's help, got a hold on the second ledge and pulled himself up.

"Good for you!" said Chad, and jumped with all his might. Being a head taller than Clive, he was able to grasp the ledge and the others helped him up. Chad sat upon the ledge with his legs dangling and looked down.

"That's all right," he said in his quiet way.

"All right for an hour," replied the girl in an equally quiet voice. Chad looked at her, then at the cliff. He nodded.

"I see what you mean. The tide comes over this ledge."

"A good six feet above it," was the girl's reply. Chad stood up, faced the cliff, studied it for a while, then spoke to Clive.

"I think we can pull her up high enough to be safe." The girl heard.

"Don't worry about me," she retorted. "I can climb as well as you." Chad smiled. He liked her pluck.

"Come on then," he said.

The three scrambled along the ledge. It was very narrow and very slippery, and by this time rain was coming down in torrents. The roar of the waves just below them almost drowned the thunder, and spray, leaping up, stung their faces. Chad stopped and pointed to a projecting knob of rock. He reached up, got hold of it and drew himself up. Then he pulled the girl up and afterwards Clive. Above them was a deep niche running slantingly upwards. There was room at the bottom for all three and, crouching in it, they found shelter from the driving rain.

"We're above high water mark," Chad said.

"We're safe here," the girl agreed. She looked at Chad. "It was nice of you to come after me. I'm frightfully sorry you lost your boat."

"Better than losing our lives," Chad said gravely. "Now do you mind telling me what you were doing on that ledge?"

"I was looking for the Plunder Pit," the girl replied.

CHAPTER II

THE BLACK HOLE

IT was such a surprising answer that Clive and Chad both stared at her without saying anything. The girl laughed, and she had a very nice laugh.

"It's quite true," she went on. "My name is Wanda Heriot, and I live at Badger's Holt, which is just over the hill, facing the river. It's a very old house, and my people have lived there for hundreds of years. Now there's no one left except Dad and me, and he is crippled. We are pretty hard up and have to take paying guests in order to keep things going. There's a story that an ancestor of ours, Alured Heriot, who was a privateer, hid a lot of valuables in a cellar or cave called the Plunder Pit. Dad believes the story is true, but we've looked and looked and never found anything. To-day I went off on my own and climbed along the foot of the cliff. I thought there might be some hole or cave that one couldn't see from a boat. Then I got caught by the storm." She shrugged. "I should have been drowned if you hadn't come. It was awfully brave of you. I only wish we could pay for your boat."

"Don't worry about the boat," Clive said quickly. "She was insured, so we can get a new one. But we're frightfully interested about this treasure. I didn't know there were such things in England. Couldn't we help you to look for it?" Wanda looked doubtful. Chad spoke.

"Clive is right. We're on holiday and we'd love a bit of excitement like this. We're quite respectable. Clive's father is Charles Medland, a well known barrister. My name is Chadwyck Lamerton, and my dad has a place called Wansdyke, in Somerset. We're staying at Bulport and were out fishing when the storm came. Now what about it?"

"It would be splendid," said Wanda earnestly, then stopped and looked down at the raging sea. "But how are we going to get back?" she asked.

"Won't someone come with a boat," Clive asked; "after the storm, I mean?"

"No one knows I came here," said Wanda. Clive whistled softly.

"That's a bit awkward." Then he brightened. "But we can get back the way you came."

"You're forgetting the tide," Wanda said. "It was full ebb when I started." Clive whistled again.

"You're right, Wanda. I'd clean forgotten the tide. Then we're stuck here till to-morrow morning. It won't be much fun, sitting here all night in our wet things."

"It isn't that I'm thinking of," said Wanda. "It's Dad and John Otter and Rachel. They'll be terrified when I don't come back."

"Who's John Otter?"

"Our man. Rachel's his wife. They look after the house."

"Won't John come to look for you?" Clive asked.

"Yes, but he will think I am up on the moor. I didn't tell him or anyone where I was going. Dad hates my going on the cliffs." Clive shook his head.

"It's a bit of a mess. But I'll tell you what. When the sea goes down I'll swim round."

"You can't," said Wanda flatly. "There's a tremendous current out of the harbour. Besides, the wind won't go down before dark."

"Oh, hang!" exclaimed Clive impatiently, "but we've got to do something." Chad, who had been listening all this time without putting in a word, spoke.

"I'll climb the cliff," he said.

"Climb the cliff!" Wanda repeated. "Could you?"

"I think I could," Chad said in his quiet way. "You and Clive could stay here and I'd fetch Otter and a rope and then you could both get up easily." Wanda scrambled to her feet.

"I've been climbing about these cliffs since I was ten," she said. "If you go, I'm going, too."

Chad didn't like it, but saw that Wanda meant what she said. He saw, too, that she was slim and strong and active as a boy, and he knew already that she could keep her head.

"All right," he said at last. "The rain's nearly over. Let's go."

The start was the worst part of it, for they had to worm their way up the niche, or chimney, which was almost straight up and down and had very few handholds. Chad went first, Wanda next and Clive last. Without Chad they would never have got up at all. Chad, though not quite fifteen, was five foot eight, broad-shouldered and tremendously strong. Besides all that, he knew much more about rock climbing than the others.

The chimney ran up for about twenty feet, and when they got to the top they found a broad ledge where they rested and got breath. This ledge slanted upwards to the left and they went along it until it broke off short in a gap about six feet wide. They looked straight down into the heaving waves.

"We can't go any further," said Wanda.

"Oh, I don't know," Chad answered; then, before the others realized what he was about, he made a great spring and landed safely on the far side. Wanda's face went white.

"I can't follow," she gasped. Chad turned.

"Don't try," he said coolly. "There's another ledge above. I can reach it from here, then I'll pull you up." Up he went like a great cat, and next minute they saw his head just above them. Wanda stretched up her arms, he caught her and dragged her up; then, as soon as she was safe beside him, hauled up Clive.

"I wouldn't have jumped that gap for—for the treasure itself," Wanda said.

"Anyone can jump six feet," Chad said with a laugh. "We're past the worst. See! It's quite easy now."

It wasn't exactly easy, but from that point on the climb was not nearly so difficult, and soon they were more than half way to the top. They were scrambling along a ledge which led steeply upwards and Chad, still leading, had just squeezed round a projecting boulder, when he stopped short.

"What's up?" Wanda asked. Chad turned and helped her round the corner.

"Looking for a cave, weren't you?" he said, and pointed to the mouth of a tunnel which opened in the cliff face just in front. Wanda drew a quick breath.

"A cave! Oh, let me see." She stepped quickly past Chad and went straight into the mouth of the black hole. Chad stepped after her and caught her by the arm.

"Steady, Wanda! It's not safe—not in the dark." Wanda turned to him. Her dark blue eyes were shining, and her face was alight with eagerness.

"We must search," she exclaimed. "It may be the Plunder Pit. Haven't you got some matches?" Chad put a hand into the pocket of his grey flannel jacket and pulled out a box. He took out a match and tried to strike it, but there was not even a spark.

"All wet," he said. "Sorry, Wanda, but we shall have to wait until to-morrow."

CHAPTER III

THE BIG MAN

WANDA stood a moment, gazing into the depths of the black hole in the cliff. Chad could see that she was very disappointed and he liked her all the better because she didn't say so. Instead she turned to him and Clive.

"And you're as wet as the matches, so the sooner we get home the better. Come on. The rest looks easy."

The climb may have looked easy, and it was easy compared with what they had done already. All the same, it was a tough scramble, and all three were glad when they reached the top.

"There's our house," said Wanda pointing, and both boys pulled up short.

The storm had passed, and the sun, breaking through the dark clouds, lit up a long slope which dropped to what looked like a small lake but was really the mouth of the Badger Brook. Half way down this slope stood an old grey house almost covered with honeysuckle and Virginia creeper. A terraced garden ran down to the water's edge where a boat lay at a landing. Beyond were miles and miles of moor rising to great hills in the distance, and here and there could be seen the brook tumbling down from the heights in falls and long stickles.

"It's fine!" said Chad, and the admiration in his voice brought a smile to Wanda's face.

"Top hole," Clive agreed.

"It's a dear old place," Wanda answered, "but it isn't much fun living in a big house like that when there's no money to keep it up. That's why I'm so keen to find this treasure." She turned to Chad and her face was glowing. "I believe that's the way to it—that cave, I mean."

"I hope it is," Chad said. "Anyhow we'll find out before we're much older. Your father will be quite excited."

Wanda raised a hand.

"You must not say a word to him, Chad. Or you, Clive. I don't want a word said about that cave until we've explored it."

Chad nodded.

"I see. We'll be mum. But you know I think you're right, Wanda. I mean about that hole being the mouth of the treasure cave. The opening is almost on a level with the house, and exactly the other side of the bluff. And it seems to run in the right direction."

"I do hope you're right," Wanda said earnestly. "But let's hurry. We shall all catch colds if we stand about here in the wind."

"Don't know what we're going to do about clothes," Clive whispered to Chad. "We're in no state to pay an afternoon call."

Wanda overheard.

"Don't bother about that. Rachel will manage. And you're so big, Chad, you can wear one of Dad's suits. We'll go in the back way, then Dad won't see how wet we are."

At the back door a woman met them. A big, motherly woman with the deep chest and creamy skin of a native of Devon.

"Oh! Miss Wanda, I'm surely glad to see you," she exclaimed. "Jan and I were getting proper anxious. And you out in all that storm!"

"I'm quite all right, Rachel," Wanda assured her. "Though I mightn't have been but for these boys. This is Mr. Chadwyck Lamerton and the other is Mr. Clive Medland. I got stuck on a ledge and they came and helped me, and their boat was wrecked. And please light a fire in the Blue room, Rachel. We must get them dry things, too." Rachel Otter gave the boys one quick look. It seemed to satisfy her. She nodded.

"I'll see to it, Miss Wanda. They'd better stay by the kitchen fire while I fix things up. And you go change them wet things at once."

"Good sort," said Chad when he and Clive were left alone in the warm kitchen.

"She's all of that," agreed Clive. "So is Wanda. Strikes me we're in luck, old man." Chad smiled in his quiet way.

"It does look as if we were in for a bit of fun. Quite a good scheme if we can find this treasure."

"We're jolly well going to," Clive declared. And just then Rachel came back.

"I've lighted the fire in the Blue room. Will you come up, young gentlemen?" They followed her. The house was big and airy and they passed through a finely panelled hall. The Blue room was on the first floor. A cheerful fire was blazing and on the bed lay a variety of clothes.

"They're old things of the master's," Rachel explained. "Jan shall fetch your suit cases from Bulport before night."

"Tell him we're awfully obliged to him," said Chad as he sat down to scribble a note to the hotel-keeper.

It was pleasant to strip off their sopping clothes, have a good rub down with rough towels and get into dry things. Chad found a pair of flannel trousers and an old tweed coat which did him very well, but Clive had to take several reefs in his trousers. However, he was too excited about the treasure to worry about his appearance, and when Wanda tapped at the door, he and Chad were quite ready to go down. Wanda had changed into a blue frock which suited her fair hair and complexion. She was a very pretty girl.

"Tea is in the dining-room," she said, "and mind—not a word of the cave!"

Mr. Heriot looked very frail. But there was no mistake about the warmth with which he greeted the boys.

"Wanda has told me how you saved her," he

said. "It was a fine piece of work. What grieves me is that you should have lost your boat."

"Don't worry about that, sir," Chad said. "What's worrying us is planting ourselves on you like this." Mr. Heriot smiled.

"I'm delighted to have you, and I hope you will stay as long as you can. Wanda hardly sees anyone of her own age."

Before Chad could reply, the door opened and a man came in. The boys stared. They couldn't help it.

The newcomer was simply huge. He was not only tall but stout. He would weigh at least sixteen stone, Chad thought. He had a big, smooth face, small, very bright blue eyes and his hands and feet were enormous. He was in fishing kit, a suit of check tweeds with thick stockings and heavy brogues. Seeing the boys he pulled up and stared at them.

"Hulloa!" he said in a voice that matched his size, "company to tea."

CHAPTER IV

THE RIFT

MR. HERIOT introduced the boys.

"These are Chadwyck Lamerton and Clive Medland, Mr. Torgan. Friends of Wanda. I hope you had good sport."

"Not so dusty," Torgan answered. "Fourteen trout, and two are over the pound. I'll lay I've beaten Garnett to-day."

"A man who fishes with a worm can always beat one who fishes with a fly," came a sharp voice. Its owner, who had followed Torgan into the room, was a thick-set, square shouldered, upright man with a close-cut moustache and hard grey eyes.

"There's no law against using a worm, Garnett," retorted Torgan. "And what else would you use with the water coming down as thick as it did after that storm?"

"If you cannot catch trout with a fly, you should leave them alone," said Garnett curtly. "No sportsman uses bait for trout."

"You're jealous, Garnett. That's the trouble with you," jeered Torgan. "Even if you had the worms you wouldn't know how to use them."

"Worms!" began Garnett furiously, but Mr. Heriot cut in.

"Since I have no objection to the use of worms, Major Garnett, I don't think you need protest," he said quietly. "After all, there are plenty of trout for both. Let me introduce two young friends of Wanda." Major Garnett nodded curtly to the boys, and they all sat down to tea. There were splits with rich yellow clotted cream and strawberry jam, saffron cakes and rock cakes, while for anyone who was really hungry there was home-baked bread and home-made butter.

Chad and Clive, who had not eaten since breakfast, thoroughly enjoyed their tea. Afterwards Wanda showed the boys the house.

"Those two guests of yours must be a bit trying, Wanda," said Clive.

"They're always quarrelling," Wanda answered, tossing her head. "But Dad and I don't pay much attention. The cellars are down here," she went on as she gained a door. "Wait till I get a candle."

She got one from the pantry and led the way down a steep flight of steps into a large cellar, three walls of which were of solid rock, but the fourth, the one opposite the stairs, of masonry. Wanda went across, reached up and pressed a stone and at once a big block rolled back with a slight grating sound, leaving a narrow opening in the wall.

"A secret door!" cried Clive. "Is this the treasure chamber, Wanda?"

"No, only a second cellar."

"That's a wonderfully clever bit of machinery for moving the stone," said Chad.

"Dad says it's the same sort that the old Aztecs used in Mexico," Wanda told him. "It shows that our pirate ancestor must have lived there."

"Then surely there's another opening out of this place," Chad argued as they went through into the second cellar. Wanda shook her head.

"There isn't. Or if there is I can't find it, and I've spent hours and hours hunting for it."

"Then it looks as if someone must have gone off with the stuff," Clive said.

"But I was the first to find the way in here," Wanda answered. "No one had any idea of this second cellar until I just happened to touch the right stone." Chad frowned.

"It's funny. But never mind, Wanda. To-morrow we'll go to the cave and, if there is any-thing in this treasure story, I feel sure we shall find it."

"Oh, I do hope we can," said Wanda eagerly. "It would make all the difference in the world. Dad is dreading that he may have to sell Badger's Holt."

"Sell this place!" said Chad sharply. "You couldn't. It would be simply awful."

"Perfectly awful!" Clive agreed. Chad began poking about the cellar and trying the walls, but the floor and walls both seemed to be all solid rock, so presently they went up and began to collect the things they would need for their expedition next day. Chad said they must have a crowbar and a rope as well as candles, and Wanda found these and they hid them in an outhouse.

"I don't want anyone to know where we are going," Wanda told the boys. "Don't say a word about the treasure to Dad or anybody else."

"Do you think anyone else is after it?" Chad asked.

"I don't see how that's possible," said Wanda, "because no one else knows. You two are the only people I've talked to except Jan and Rachel."

Next morning was gloriously fine, and Wanda told her father that she and the boys were taking their lunch out. They had agreed to leave at ten, but at that hour Wanda would not start because Mr. Torgan was still hanging about.

"We must wait until he has gone off fishing," she said. "I don't want him to see where we are going."

"I can't fancy him cave hunting," grinned Clive. "He's so big, he'd stick."

"I'm not taking any risks," Wanda said firmly, and actually it was nearly twelve before the three left. So far as they could tell, no one saw them climb the hill, and once they were over the top they were out of sight of the house. Reaching a spot above the cave, Chad pounded the crowbar into the turf and tied the rope to it. Holding on to the rope they all went down quite easily.

The first part of the cave was high enough to walk upright, but a little way in, the roof came down so low they had to crawl. The floor was very wet and slippery but the air seemed fairly fresh. After creeping a little distance, they came to a rock chamber, which was about ten feet high and twenty feet across. Chad stooped and picked up something from the floor.

"What is it—what have you got?" Wanda asked quickly.

"A shoe buckle," Chad said slowly. "Pretty old-fashioned, too." Wanda took the rusty bit of metal. She drew a quick breath.

"It is a buckle. Yes, and awfully old. Oh, Chad, this makes me sure that we are on the right track."

"Don't get excited," Chad said quietly. "We'll soon see." He went on again, picking his way among great chunks of rock which had fallen from the roof, but had not gone far before he pulled up short.

"What's the matter?" Clive demanded, pushing forward. Chad thrust out a big arm and stopped him.

"Steady, Clive. Keep back, Wanda." He held up his candle and its light showed a great rift in the floor which ran from wall to wall. He picked up a stone and dropped it over the edge. It seemed an age before the sound of a sullen splash came up out of the black depths. Chad turned to Wanda.

"Goes clean down to sea level," he said. "And it's too wide to jump." Wanda looked dreadfully disappointed.

"You mean we can't go any further, Chad?"

"Not to-day," Chad answered quietly.

CHAPTER V

TORGAN TALKS OF POACHERS

CLIVE stepped forward to the edge of the gap. "I believe I could jump it," he said.

"You're not going to try, my son," Chad told him. "And anyhow, Wanda can't. We'll need a plank, and a good big one, to get across."

"Jan will get us one. Let's go back for it at once," said Wanda.

"Come on," Clive said eagerly, and started back.

Jan was at work in the garden. He was a heavy-set man—"stuggy" as they say in Devonshire—and his pleasant face was burnt almost to walnut colour by sun and wind. Wanda explained what she wanted and he nodded.

"There's a plank in tool house as might do, Missy. But her's heavy. I'll have to help 'ee get her over the hill." Wanda looked doubtful.

"We don't want anyone to see us, Jan. Where is Mr. Torgan?"

"Went fishing. Baint back yet far as I know." He looked at Wanda. "You don't trust that gentleman, Missy?"

"Not when it comes to this treasure, Jan," Wanda answered.

"You'm right," Jan agreed as he stuck his spade into the ground and started towards the tool shed. The plank was a huge thing, and Chad saw at once that he and Clive could not carry it. Jan suggested that he should saw a piece off it, and Chad agreed.

"The gap's about eight feet wide," he said, "so if the plank is ten, that ought to be plenty." Jan got a saw and set to work. He had just finished when Wanda, who had been standing outside, came in.

"Mr. Torgan is coming back," she said in a very annoyed tone. "He is fishing the long pool. We shall have to wait until he is in the house before we start."

"Then I'll get back to my digging, Missy," Jan said. "You call me soon as her's out o' sight."

They waited and waited, but Torgan was slow as a snail. He fished every yard of the long pool. At last he came to the end, and they waited for him to start back to the house. Imagine their disgust when they saw him turn back to the upper end and start fishing the pool down a second time!

"He didn't catch anything either," said Wanda.

"Do you think he's watching us?" Clive asked.

"I don't know what to think," Wanda answered frowning. Chad looked at his watch.

"It's nearly four, Wanda. Too late to get that plank to the cave before tea." Wanda bit her lip.

"It's too bad. Now we shall have to wait till to-morrow."

"Tell you what," said Chad. "I'll slip out after tea and Jan and I will carry the plank to the top of the cliff. Then we can start early to-morrow."

Wanda brightened.

"That would help, Chad. But all the same, I'm dreadfully disappointed. Finding that shoe buckle makes me quite sure we are on the right track. Now we'd better go in and get ready for tea."

Tea was at half-past four, and Torgan was there as well as Major Garnett.

"Hulloa, youngsters, what have you been up to?" Torgan cried jovially.

"Picnicking," Wanda answered politely.

"Where did you go?" continued Torgan.

"Up on the hill," said Wanda vaguely; then Major Garnett struck in.

"Perhaps you'd like to know where I went," he said sarcastically.

"I don't need to ask," retorted Torgan. "I'll lay you spent the whole day on Pixie's Pool. Trust you to collar the best fishing water."

"At any rate I was fishing with a fly," said Garnett sourly.

"Are you sure it wasn't a minnow?" asked Torgan.

"It was *not* a minnow. I never use one of those filthy things with a dozen hooks on it. In my opinion it's worse than worm fishing. But some people would use anything—even dynamite." Torgan burst out laughing, and the Major, very offended, got up and left the room. Torgan turned to his host.

"Sorry," he said, "but I never can help pulling Garnett's leg. He takes everything so seriously."

"All the more reason why you should be considerate towards him, Mr. Torgan," said Mr. Heriot quietly. Torgan took no offence.

"I know. I must try and remember," he said. He changed the subject. "Oh, I'd almost forgotten. I met old Ben Caunter and he told me there are some gipsy chaps on the moor. Queer looking fellows, he said. I only hope they don't start poaching your water, Mr. Heriot."

"I don't think we need trouble about them," Mr. Heriot replied. "They may take a few trout for their supper, but I've never had any serious poaching. Certainly not dynamiting," he added with a smile. Torgan shrugged.

"Well, I thought I'd tell you," he said, and got up. "I must put my rod away," he remarked and went out.

The others stayed and talked a while to Mr. Heriot, then Chad excused himself and went off to find Jan. The evening had turned dull and misty, and the two got the plank, carried it to the top of the hill and hid it in a gorse clump.

"Do you think there's any truth in the treasure story, Jan?" Chad asked as they walked back.

"The master believes in un," Jan answered. "He've got some old papers as tells the story. Aye, I wouldn't wonder if 'twere true, and I surely hopes you finds un. It would just about break the old gentleman's heart if he had to sell this here place."

"Bad as that, is it?" Chad asked.

"It surely is. Things been going downhill terrible of late. If it weren't for these here paying guests—as they calls 'em—us couldn't get along at all."

"Do you think anyone else is on the track, Jan?" Chad enquired. Jan's sharp eyes probed Chad's face.

"You'm of the same opinion as Miss Wanda, I'm thinking."

"She does seem suspicious," said Chad, "but she hasn't said much." Jan frowned.

"I don't know what to think, Mr. Chad. There's funny things going on. Folk walks about by night. I baint easy in my mind." He stopped short. "There be the Major. Best not say more. Voices do carry in this quiet air." Chad saw Major Garnett striding up the hill with a pipe in his mouth.

"Is it going to rain, Otter?" he called out.

"More like fog, sir," said Jan; and Garnett came over and walked with them down to the house.

CHAPTER VI

NOISE IN THE NIGHT

THAT night Chad lay awake, thinking things over. Though he had known the Heriots for less than forty-eight hours, he felt as if they were old friends, and he was desperately keen to help them. What bothered him about this business was that, if the treasure really was hidden somewhere underground, there would surely be some way to the hiding place from the house.

Wanda had already found one hidden cellar. It seemed to him that there must be another, or at any rate some passage from one of the two cellars into the heart of the hill. He resolved that if they found nothing in the cave, he would have another hunt in the cellars. What he was most afraid of was that the treasure had been in that second cellar and that someone had found and gone off with it years ago. Wondering whether this was the case, Chad drifted off into dreamland, and the next thing he knew someone was shaking him awake.

"Chad! Chad!" It was Clive's voice. "Wake up!" Chad sat up quickly.

"What's up?" he said in a sharp whisper.

"I don't know. I heard something. A sort

of clang. I got up and went to the head of the stairs, and heard someone moving below. Thought I'd better tell you." Chad was out of bed like a shot.

"All right. Don't suppose it was anything out of the way, but we'd just as well have a look-see. Did you see any lights?" he went on as he pushed his feet into a pair of slippers.

"No. That's what made me suspicious. If it was someone in the house going down for anything, they'd have had a candle."

"That's true," said Chad as he made for the door.

"We'll go down," he whispered, and started down the stairs. Silent as a ghost, Clive followed. Below all was quiet. There was no light and no sound of anyone moving. Chad made along the passage into the back regions. He tried the back door and found it fast. Then he tried the cellar door, but that, too, was locked. They returned to the front door, but it was both locked and bolted. All the windows in the sitting-rooms were closed. They came back into the hall and Clive spoke.

"This beats me, Chad. The noise was loud enough to wake me, so I certainly didn't dream it. Besides, I heard someone moving after I went out on the landing."

"It must have been Torgan or Garnett," Chad told him. "One of them might have come down for a book or something he'd forgotten."

"I suppose you're right," Clive answered slowly. Do you think we ought to knock up Jan?"

"No. Jan works jolly hard, and he has to be up at six. What time is it now?"

"It was just after two when I woke," Clive said.

"Better go back to bed, Clive. I'll hang around a while and if I hear anything I'll call you."

After Clive had gone to his room, Chad sat on a chair just inside the open door of his own room and waited for quite a long time. Nothing happened and at last, feeling rather chilly, he climbed into bed again and was soon asleep.

For a second time he was roused abruptly—this time by a sharp knock on his door.

"Chad! May I come in?" cried Wanda.

"Yes, come in," he called as he sat up. Wanda came in. She wore a blue dressing gown. Her face was pale and her eyes full of fright.

"Jan has gone!" she told him.

"Jan gone!" repeated Chad in a dazed voice. "Where?"

"That's what none of us know. Rachel woke up to find he was gone from their room. She didn't think anything of it because he often gets up early to light the fire for her. She dressed and came down, but there was no fire and the blinds were still down and the doors were locked. Then she got frightened and searched all round. There wasn't a sign of him, and she came up to tell me."

Chad was wide awake now.

"Then that's what Clive heard," he said sharply. He told her quickly of the sound in the night.

"But I don't understand," said Wanda, bewildered. "You say the doors were all locked. How did Jan get out of the house?"

"I don't know any more than you, Wanda. Go and tell Clive. Tell him to dress quickly. I'll be down in five minutes."

Five minutes later Chad, Clive and Wanda were searching the house, but it did not take them long to make certain that Jan was not in it. Then they went out the back way and tried the out-buildings, the cow-shed, the garden. Again not a sign of the missing man. They came back to the kitchen where Rachel was waiting. Rachel was very badly frightened, yet amazingly brave. So far from giving way, she had lighted the fire and put on the kettle. Chad told her how Clive and he had gone round the house in the night.

"Jan must have heard the noise and gone down," he said. "Perhaps someone was trying to break in."

"But how did he get out of the house, Mr. Chad?" Rachel questioned. "He wouldn't have waited to lock the door behind him. Besides, they were all locked on the inside." Chad shook his head. This was a question he could not answer. Nor could Clive or Wanda find any reply. As they stood gazing at one another dumbly, the door opened, and the tall figure of Mr. Torgan appeared.

"What's the matter?" he demanded. "Why are you all running about the house at this hour? It isn't seven yet." Chad told him what had happened.

"Jan Otter gone!" repeated Torgan amazed. "And all the doors locked on the inside. Why, it's impossible!"

"It may be impossible, but it's true," said Chad curtly. Torgan looked from one to the other. "He must have got through a window."

"They were all closed, too. At least the downstairs ones," said Wanda. "Didn't you hear anything in the night, Mr. Torgan?"

"Not a sound. Never opened an eye until I heard you people running about." Again he looked round. "Has anyone looked for footmarks?" he asked suddenly. "No—well I'm going out to see if I can find any." He hurried off.

Rachel dropped on a chair.

"Oh, what shall I do?" she said. Wanda took charge.

"You'll have a cup of tea," she said firmly. "And you're not to worry. Jan is all right. I'm sure of that." She got the caddy and set to making the tea. At the same time she signed to the boys to leave the kitchen. They slipped out. Both were feeling quite dazed. The front door was open and they went outside. Next minute Torgan came hurrying back.

"The boat's gone," he said. "And there are footmarks by the landing, which I'm pretty sure are Otter's."

CHAPTER VII

THE EMPTY BOAT

CHAD and Clive ran down to the landing. Sure enough, the boat had vanished. Torgan, coming up behind, pointed to footprints on the sandy shore. Chad examined them.

"There's been more than one man here," he said, "and some of these marks are much bigger than those of Jan's feet." Torgan frowned thoughtfully.

"I believe you're right. Then it looks as if Otter followed some man or men down here and they caught him and took him away in the boat."

"But how did he get out of the house?" Clive demanded. "As Rachel said, he wouldn't have stopped to lock the door behind him. In any case both the front and back door keys were on the inside of the doors." Torgan was still frowning.

"He must have gone out of a window. Listen! Supposing he heard something and looked out. He sees a couple of chaps trying to get in. He knows they'll see or hear him if he goes out by the doors, so he slips out of a window. They spot him all the same, knock him on the head and carry him off. They stick him in the boat and turn it adrift."

"That sounds pretty thin to me," Chad said bluntly. "In the first place, if Jan had got out of a window he'd have left it open so he could get back; and in the second, if these men had hit him over the head, surely they wouldn't have bothered to carry him all the way down to the landing! They'd have left him and hooked it."

"And why would they have tried to get into the house?" added Clive. "There's nothing worth stealing." Torgan took no offence.

"They might have been netting the river," he suggested. "That would have started Otter after them about as quickly as anything."

"That's true enough," Chad said, "but it doesn't explain the closed window." Torgan grew impatient.

"Well, the man's gone, so he must have got out some way." Chad nodded. There was no answer to this. Torgan went on: "Best thing we can do is to inform the police. If Mr. Heriot is agreeable I'll take my car and run over to Bulport."

"That's a good notion, sir," Chad said. "And you might tell them to warn the coast-guards and ask them to look for the boat," Clive spoke:

"How would it be if you and I went up the cliff, Chad, to see if we could spot it?"

"We could do that," Chad agreed, "but first we'd better see Mr. Heriot."

Wanda had already told her father what had happened. She had taken charge, and was helping

Rachel to get breakfast ready. Rachel was wonderfully plucky, but her pale face and reddened eyes showed how she was suffering. Major Garnett was down. To Wanda's surprise he was quite kind, and asked if he could be of any use.

Breakfast was a silent meal. They none of them felt like discussing Jan's disappearance, but Mr. Heriot agreed that the police should be informed, and Torgan drove off almost at once in his car. Then Chad and Clive went up the cliff. The tide had been ebbing at two o'clock, so the boat would probably have drifted out to sea, but it was making now, and Chad thought that the boat might be stranded in some little cove. There was very little wind, but what there was came from the west. It promised to be a very hot day.

Chad was right. About two miles down the coast they spotted the boat lying high and dry on the shingle of a small cove. They managed to climb down the steep cliff and found that the boat was quite uninjured and that the oars were still in it. But of Jan there was no sign at all. The two looked at one another.

"This beats me," said Clive. "If Jan had been in the boat he wouldn't have left it here, and if anyone else had been in it, this is about the last place they'd have landed. One thing is sure. They'd never have got up those cliffs in the dark." Chad nodded.

"You're right, Clive, and I'm as puzzled as you. I don't believe Jan was ever in the boat."

"You mean that it was set adrift as a blind."

"It looks like it," said Chad, "yet it doesn't make sense. I've been racking my brains for some explanation, but the more I think the more muddled I get." He looked at the boat. "I suppose we'd better take it back. We can look at the coast on the way and see if Jan is stranded anywhere." They dragged the boat down, launched it and pulled back, but there wasn't a sign of anything living except gulls. As they passed under the great headland which they had climbed in the storm two days earlier, Chad stopped pulling.

"I can't help thinking, Clive, that this business is somehow tied up with the treasure."

"I've thought of that, myself," Clive answered. "But for the life of me I don't see how."

"You said you heard a clang in the night, Clive," Chad said slowly. "I've been wondering if it was that cellar door." Clive started.

"By jove, that was it! Come to think of it, it was just the sound that door does make. It's very heavy, and there's a sort of echo when it closes."

"Then we'd best go and look at it as soon as ever we get back." He took hold of his oar as he spoke.

"Just a minute," said Clive. "If it was that door, is it your notion that someone has found a way into the house through the cellars?"

"That's the idea." Clive shook his head.

"Even supposing these chaps did get into the cellars from outside, why would they want to go through the house?"

"I don't say they would," replied Chad. "What I think is that Jan heard them and opened the cellar door. Then they collared him."

"And took him out the back way?"

"Yes—and afterwards turned the boat loose as a blind." Clive considered a moment.

"That would account for the front and back doors being still locked, but not for the cellar door."

"Was the key in the cellar door?"

"I don't remember."

"We'll find out when we get back," Clive said, and set to pulling.

Wanda was at the landing to meet them.

"Have you found Jan?" was her first eager question. They told her where they had found the boat, and Clive explained Chad's idea.

"The key wasn't in the cellar door," Wanda said quickly.

"Then it looks as if Chad's notion might be the right one," Clive said. "Let's go down to the cellars and have another look round."

They found the cellar key hanging in its usual place in the kitchen and this time took three candles so as to be sure of having plenty of light. They locked the door behind them so that no one could see what they were about, and they searched the two cellars—every inch of them—but found absolutely nothing.

As they came up again a car arrived.

"It's Torgan," said Clive.

"And he's brought a policeman," Wanda added quickly. "No," she added, "it isn't just a policeman. It's Sergeant Eve."

CHAPTER VIII

A SECOND SEARCH

SERGEANT EVE was tall, stiff and dark. He asked a great many questions and especially of Rachel.

"Did your husband come up to bed before you were asleep?" he asked.

"We came up the same time, sir. We nearly always do."

"You went to sleep at once?"

"Yes," said Rachel. "And so did Jan."

"And you never woke till morning?"

Rachel agreed.

"Then your husband might have gone out any time in the night without your knowing it?" Again Rachel said yes. Eve let Rachel go and then questioned Clive about the sounds he had heard. Clive was quite definite. He had heard a sound like a door being closed.

"And it was loud enough to wake you. It seems funny it didn't rouse anyone else except perhaps John Otter."

"My room is nearest the stairs, and my door was ajar," Clive told him. Eve questioned everyone in the house, including Wanda, then went into Mr. Heriot's study and talked to him for some time. Afterwards Torgan drove him back. Wanda went in to see her father and came out, looking very bothered.

"The sergeant thinks Jan went off on his own account," she said indignantly to the boys. "Did you ever hear such nonsense?"

"Went off on his own account?" Clive repeated. "I don't understand."

"He thinks he's run away. He believes that Rachel let him out and locked the door behind him. He asked Dad if anything was missing."

"Silly ass!" growled Clive. "I bet your father sent him off with a flea in his ear."

"Yes, Dad told him that Jan was not only his servant but his friend, and that he would as soon suspect himself as he would Jan. So Eve got his back up and said stiffly that he would make enquiries and notify other stations."

"Fat lot of good that will do!" Clive exclaimed angrily. "If Jan's to be found, we've got to find him ourselves."

"That is my opinion also." The three turned in surprise to see Major Garnett standing behind them.

"Yes, Medland, that policeman is a fool," the Major continued in his precise voice. "I am inclined to think that Otter has either been taken by force or decoyed away. I have spent the morning in investigations of my own and this is what I have found." He took from his pocket an old-fashioned, coloured cotton handkerchief and held it out. Wanda took it quickly.

"It's Jan's," she said. "Where—where did you find it, Major Garnett?"

"Hanging in a gorse bush just beyond the bridge over the stream. It looks to me as if Otter had thrown or dropped it there on purpose. I did my best to find tracks, but was unable to do so. But your eyes are sharper than mine and it may be that you would be more successful. At any rate, the effort would be worth while."

"We'll have a try, anyhow," said Chad. "We'd better get along at once, Clive. All the same, I wish I knew which way to go." The Major glanced round as if to make sure no one was listening.

"My own impression is that the men who caught Otter were poachers. In that case they would probably have some camp in that wild stretch of moor to the south. If I were you I should climb the high ridge that is called Tor Royal. From there you get a wide view. I would accompany you, but unfortunately my wounded leg is troubling me."

Wanda put up some sandwiches for them, and ten minutes later Chad and Clive were walking briskly towards the bridge which crossed the brook just above the harbour.

They crossed the bridge and began to examine the ground, but the heat of the previous day had dried it pretty thoroughly, and in any case it was all grass and heather. They found no marks, so pushed straight on towards Tor Royal.

It was rough going and the heat was intense.

They took off their coats and carried them and plugged along up hill and down, making for the mighty ridge that towered against the skyline to the south.

In the wide hollow below the Tor lay a great bog where acres of liquid slime glistened like black ink in the sun blaze. The boys had to make a wide swing to the east to clear this. At the eastern end was a stretch of soft ground and, as they crossed his, Chad pulled up short and pointed to footmarks in the peat. Both boys stooped and examined them.

"Three sets," said Chad. "One very big, one very broad and the third—Clive, these marks are just about Jan's size." Clive's eyes were bright as he looked at the marks.

"Just about," he agreed eagerly. "'Pon my Sam, it looks as if the Major was right and that Jan had been kidnapped." Chad frowned.

"But what for? What in the name of sense could anyone want with Jan?"

"They might think he knows where the treasure is," Clive suggested.

"But how could *they* know anything about the treasure?" Chad demanded. "Wanda told us that she hadn't said a word to anyone but Jan and ourselves. And if she says so, you may bet it's true." Clive shrugged.

"It's no use making guesses. What we have to do is to find Jan. Let's see if we can follow these tracks."

"Only thing we can do," Chad agreed, "but I doubt if they'll carry us far." In this he was right, for, once off the soft ground, it would have taken a bloodhound to follow the trail over sheep-bitten turf, rocks and heather.

So at last they turned and made for the top of the ridge and by the time they reached it their shirts were sticking to their backs. On the summit, however, they met a little breeze, and both dropped on a boulder and sat facing it, getting their breath back.

The view was enormous. They could see right across the moor to the "in-country" beyond, while to the west they got a sight of miles of blue sea stretching to the blue horizon. They didn't waste time looking at the distances, but began to scan the moor beneath them. Clive caught Chad by the arm.

"What's that?" he said, pointing to a deep little valley about a mile away.

"An old mine house," Chad told him.

"Isn't that the sort of place——" He stopped short and drew a quick breath. "There's a man coming out—going down to the brook. See?"

CHAPTER IX

DOWN THE VEIN

"GET down," said Chad swiftly; "down behind the rock. He mustn't see us."

Both ducked behind the boulder and crouched there with their heads just above it, watching. The distance was too great to make out details. All they could see was a tiny figure, with a pail in his hand, strolling down from the mine house to the small brook that poured southwards through the valley. The man reached it, filled his pail, went back up the hill and vanished inside the ruinous looking stone building which stood on a ledge about two hundred yards from the water. They waited a long time, but nothing else happened. Clive looked at Chad.

"What about it?" he asked.

"Got to have a look," Chad said. "The job will be to do it without being spotted." Clive frowned.

"That's a fact. I can't see how we can get near without their spotting us."

"Best dodge will be to go round to the back of the hill above the mine house," Chad said. "It looks like rough ground on the top and we shall be near enough to see what sort of chaps they are, and if I'm not mistaken there's a vein down which we can crawl without being spotted."

"What's a 'vein?'" Clive demanded.

"A channel cut by a cloudburst. Look at that dark line down the hillside just beyond the mine building."

"I see. Yes, that would bring us pretty close. Come on."

"Not yet. We're both a bit fagged, and it's going to be tough work, crawling down that vein. Best thing we can do is to stop up here a bit and eat our sandwiches. It may cloud up later. There's a misty look over in the west."

"Cloud," said Clive. "I'll bet there'll be cloud. Another of those busting thunderstorms if I know anything. All right, let's lunch. I'm hungry enough."

Wanda's sandwiches were excellent; then the two slipped down the reverse side of the hill in search of water. They found a spring. It was ice-cold and most refreshing, and, after drinking, they went back to their post of observation.

It was now between three and four o'clock and, as the haze thickened, Chad decided that they might as well push on. But he warned Clive that they must not show themselves, so they worked round the back of the ridge into some thick heather and, creeping through this, got down into the low ground at the back of the hill in which the mine was.

All this took a long time, and it was nearly five before they had climbed the hill and found themselves immediately above the mine building. By this time the cloud had thickened to a sort of hot yellow haze—and feeling pretty sure that no one could see them, even if they were watching, the pair snaked along the hilltop until they reached the head of the vein.

"The very thing for us," Clive said. "It will take us within fifty yards of the building."

"Yes, but those fifty yards are all open," Chad warned him. "We may have to wait till dark after all."

"That doesn't matter so long as we get Jan," Clive declared. Chad looked at him.

"My dear chap, you surely don't imagine we can rescue Jan. It would be perfectly crazy to think of it. What earthly chance should we have against a couple of big men?" Clive looked crestfallen.

"Then what are we going to do?" he asked.

"Find out if Jan is there. If he is we go back and fetch the police."

They crept down the bottom of the vein. Some ancient cloudburst had cut the peat and gravel right down to the boulders which lay beneath the top layer of soil, and it was about the nastiest travelling that anyone could imagine. As they got further down the boulders gave way to mud, thin, black, peaty stuff which was horribly slippery. To make matters still worse, there wasn't a breath of air, and it was, if possible, hotter than ever.

It seemed to Clive that they spent half a lifetime, crawling and creeping until the vein was deep enough to allow them to walk upright, and almost as long before Chad, who was leading, signed to him to stop.

"We're about opposite the mine house," Chad whispered. "Wait till I have a look over the edge." He crept up the slippery bank and peered through the fringe of heather on top. "All clear," he said, "but we'd better wait a bit until this mist grows thicker." Clive climbed up beside him. They waited about half an hour and all the time the odd yellow haze thickened. At last Chad got up.

"Now, if you're ready, Clive," he said. "But just remember you have to follow me and not make a sound. I've a notion that these fellows we're up against are about as tough as they make them."

CHAPTER X

THE STORM BREAKS

HARDLY a sound could be heard as the two boys crept across the fifty yards which separated them from the old mine house. Indeed, the silence which brooded over the moor was uncanny.

"The silence 'ung that 'eavy you was 'alf afraid to speak." Chad found Kipling's line running through his head as he paused a moment behind a gorse bush to see what was the best line of approach. The mine house stood on a mass of reddish earth and rock, the "dump" from the mine, and had a most desolate appearance. It was built of granite and roofed with slabs of stone, some of which had slipped off.

One thing was in his favour. There was no window in the side they were approaching, so it was not likely they would be seen unless anyone came out. For another thing, the hill rose so steeply behind the house that the wall on that side was only half as high as it was in front. If he and Clive could reach the house, they could lie hidden behind it, and listen for as long as they liked without much chance of being discovered.

There was not a sound from the building, not

a sign of life, and presently they were both safe behind it. Chad pressed his ear against the wall and for a long time kept quite still. At last he dropped down beside Clive.

"Can't hear a thing," he whispered. "If it hadn't been for seeing that man, I'd never believe there was anyone here."

"Don't worry," came a jeering voice. "There's someone here all right. And been waiting for you all day." They looked up to see a tall, hard-faced man with a skin dark as a Spaniard's standing over them.

Chad was on his feet in a flash. He did not hesitate a second but charged straight at the man. The force of his rush knocked the fellow right off his feet, but as he fell he grasped Chad and pulled him down, too. Clive sprang to the rescue only to be confronted by a second man, who seized him by the collar and swung him round. This second man was shorter than the other but almost as broad as he was long. His strength was tremendous, and Clive was helpless in his grasp.

"No use your fighting, young shaver," he remarked. "Just keep still and no harm won't come to you. You got the other, Jake?"

"I got him, Ben," said the long man. "And I'll learn him to try his games on me."

"You'll leave him alone, Jake," said Ben curtly. "I don't blame him for trying to get away. Reckon you'd ha' done the same in his place." Jake dragged Chad roughly to his feet. He was scowling angrily, yet Ben, it seemed, was boss, for Jake did not carry out his threats. Ben spoke:

"You two'll come along inside and quietly, if you know what's good for you."

"Why?" demanded Chad. "What business have you to make us prisoners?"

"That's a question as I ain't answering," said Ben. "We don't mean you no harm, but you just got to stay here fer the present."

"Kidnapping us—is that your game?" Clive jeered. Ben took no offence.

"Never mind what our game is. You'll know if you live long enough." Jake broke in:

"Are you going to stand here, jawing all day?" he asked angrily.

"There ain't no hurry," replied Ben. "With this here mist no one can't see us from any distance. All the same, we'll go along in. Come on, son. It ain't no use trying to fight me. You're a lusty lad, but I could handle six like you."

For a moment there was a dangerous gleam in Chad's eyes. But it passed. What Ben said was probably true. It was no use fighting and getting hurt. He and Clive must save their strength for a better chance. He shrugged.

"All right. We'll come," he said. "But you can take it from me there'll be police after us pretty soon."

"That ain't worrying us—none whatsoever," Ben answered calmly as he led the boys round the corner and into the mine house.

Inside, the long, narrow room was very dark. The two windows were so thick with grime that they let little light through. Still there was enough to see that the place was utterly ruinous and almost bare. The only furniture was an oil stove, a few cooking pots and a couple of packing cases. There were two beds made of heather, with old horse blankets spread on them—nothing else. The floor was earth.

The narrowness of the room was the first thing that struck Chad; then he saw that there was a door in the inner wall, and realised that the mine house was divided into two rooms, an outer and an inner. Ben saw him looking at the door, and grinned.

"Yes, that's where you're going, son. You'll find a friend there already—him as you come after, I reckon." Chad bit his lip. It made him furious to think how he and Clive had run their heads into this trap. Jake chuckled nastily.

"We knowed as you'd come. Seed you top o' Tor Royal. You just walked into it." Chad went rather white. With him this was not a sign of fright but of anger. Yet he remained silent. Ben looked at Jake.

"Likely you wouldn't have done no better yourself," he remarked. "Not if you'd been in these kids' shoes." He turned to the boys. "Come right in here," he said as he opened the inner door. "You won't come to no harm if you behaves yourselves. You got Ben Grint's word for that."

It was darker still in this inner room, for the only light came through a window in the roof and that was nearly covered with rubbish and dirt. Indeed, it was so dark that it was not until the door had been slammed and locked behind them that Chad saw Jan lying stretched on a bed of heather by the wall.

"Jan!" he said quickly. "Jan, are you hurt?" Jan got up stiffly.

"So they got you two," he said bitterly. "I was feared they would, and no way of warning 'ee. No, I baint hurt, Mr. Chad—none to speak of."

"But what does it all mean, Jan?" Chad asked, bewildered. Jan came nearer.

"I reckon they wants us out of the way," he whispered. "That's how come."

"Out of the way!" repeated Chad more puzzled than ever.

"Surely," said Jan. "So us can't hinder them going arter the hoard." Chad's eyes widened. So did Clive's for that matter.

"You mean that these fellows have got wind of the treasure and want a clear field to get hold of it?" Chad asked in a sharp whisper.

"I baint got no proof, but that be my notion," Jan told him. Chad drew a long breath. He was so horrified that for the moment he could find no words. Clive was the first to speak.

"Then somehow we've got to get loose," he said and, though he kept his voice low, there was no doubt he meant it.

"Get loose," Chad repeated bitterly. "What chance have we against those two? That fellow Ben is as strong as the lot of us put together." Jan beckoned them to come closer.

"You'm right, Mr. Chad," he whispered, "us can't fight them chaps. Only thing 'll be to sneak out without them seeing us. Aye, and us can do it, I reckon. You listen to me now."

Before he could say any more the gloom was lit by a livid flash, and thunder bellowed across the moor, sending crashing echoes from tor to tor.

CHAPTER XI

A WAY OUT

"THAT'S what I were waiting for. Longer it lasts the better."

"What's your notion, Jan?" Clive whispered impatiently. "How can we dodge them?"

"I'll tell 'ee fast enough. Us can't get out front side, but us might go by back door so to speak."

"You mean that we might get through into the mine adit," Chad said. Jan nodded.

"You got the rights of it, Mr. Chad. The mouth of the adit is right behind us where they boards is nailed across. I been looking at 'em, and they be proper rotten. If us could be sure as those chaps don't interfere, it wouldn't take more'n a few minutes to break 'em off."

"The mine adit?" Clive questioned. "What's that? I thought mines went straight down into the ground."

"Not tin mines," Chad explained. "The entrance is a gallery, or passage, called an adit, which runs into the hillside and slopes upwards so as to let the water run out."

"Yes," said Clive, "but what's the good of that? We could get in there, but we can't get out again."

"Which shows how much you know about tin mines," said Chad. "There's nearly always another opening."

"Let's get about it, then," said Clive, but Jan shook his head.

"Us'll have to wait. They'll be bringing of our supper pretty soon. No use starting anything so long as they may come in on us."

"That's true," said Chad. "But this mine's pretty old, isn't it?" he added. Jan nodded.

"Her's closed down these fifty years, and won't be none too safe inside. Still, I reckon any chance is better than none."

"That it is," Clive agreed eagerly. "It makes me sick to think of Wanda and her father being raided by these fellows. And that reminds me, Jan. We haven't heard how they got you."

"I don't rightly know all as did happen," Jan said. "As I told 'ee, there's been folk walking about the house at night. Might have been that there Torgan or Major Garnett. Anyways I been sleeping with the door open. Last night I was woke by a noise, so I slips on my breeches and coat and goes down. No light anywhere, far as I could see, and all quiet as a tomb. Then all of a sudden, seems like the roof fell on my head. Next thing I knows I were laying on my back out on the moor and someone pouring cold water over me.

"It were that chap Ben Grint. He baint as bad as t'other. Then he told me I'd got to come along with him and Treslove, and if I kept my mouth shut there wouldn't no harm come to me. I weren't in no shape to make a run for it, so I went along and they brought me here. How come you to find this place, Mr. Chad?"

"Major Garnett found the handkerchief you left sticking on a gorse bush near the bridge." Jan looked puzzled.

"I didn't leave no handkerchief anywheres." Chad stared, but the quick-witted Clive answered.

"One of these men put it there just to tempt us to follow."

"Aye, that might be so," Jan agreed slowly.

"But," said Chad, "this doesn't explain how all the doors were locked on the inside when we came down."

"Baint a bit 'o use asking me, Mr. Chad. I tell 'ee I were knocked out and didn't know nothing."

"But these men, Grint and Treslove, couldn't have been inside the house," Chad insisted. "Or, if they had got in, they certainly couldn't have locked the doors *on the inside* after they left."

"That be true," Jan agreed. "It were someone inside the house as hit me. Wouldn't wonder if it were that there Torgan." Chad stared. So did Clive.

"Torgan," Chad repeated. "Do you mean, Jan, that he is after the treasure?"

"I've had the notion he been up to something for a time past," Jan answered. "Always sneaking round and listening." Chad frowned.

"Hush!" whispered Clive sharply. "They're coming in."

CHAPTER XII

DANGER

THE door from the outer room opened. Jake came in, carrying three bowls of stew; Ben Grint followed with a loaf of bread and a jug of water.

"Here's your grub," said Jake, dumping his load on the floor. "Make the most of it, for you won't get no more till morning. And don't try nothing," he added threateningly, "for I'd like nothing better than to put it across you." His fierce, dark eyes were on Chad. Plainly he had not forgotten how Chad had bowled him over. Grint cut in harshly.

"Shut your mouth, you long fool. And come on out o' this." Ben put the bread down and went out.

Clive picked up his bowl of stew, sniffed it a little suspiciously, then tasted it. His face cleared. "Rabbit, with onions and potatoes. One of those chaps knows how to cook." He set to work on the food.

The storm showed no signs of abating. The rain still drummed on the roof, and every now and then came a flash and a crash. Seemingly, Jan was right in his prophecy. There was no sign of the storm ceasing. Chad finished his stew and set the bowl down.

"Jan," he said, "there's one thing worries me. Where's our light coming from—for the mine, I mean?"

"I've a torch," said Clive quickly.

"And they've left us one candle in here," Jan added. Chad shook his head.

"It's half burned now and it'll be more than half burned by the time we get into the mine. We haven't two hours' light at best, and we may be double that time or more in the mine."

"Us'll have to chance it," Jan said soberly. "If us don't get back home afore morning, who's to say what'll happen?" Chad nodded gravely.

"All right. We'll chance it. It's getting dark now. We'd best start on those boards." Clive spoke:

"Suppose they come in for the dishes?"

"That would be awkward," Chad said. "See here, Clive, you listen at the door and if you hear them coming, give us the office." Clive went to the door, then came back.

"I can do better than that. There's a crack I can see through. They're still feeding, so I can tell you if they move." Chad's face cleared.

"Fine! Then we'll get to it, Jan."

The rain pounding on the roof quite drowned any small noises made by the two in ripping away the boards, and the boards were so rotten that this work proved even more easy than they had expected. Within less than five minutes there was an opening large enough for a man to crawl through. Sure enough, in front of them was the low-browed opening of the mine adit. Clive reported that their gaolers showed no signs of moving, so it was decided to start at once, and one by one they slipped through the opening.

Clive switched on his torch, and the light showed a low roofed tunnel. The floor was greasy mud. Walls and roof were supported by timbers, most of them rotten, and some covered with thick white fungus which shone with a ghostly phosphorescent light. The air was dank and chilly and heavy with the smell of dry rot.

The tunnel ran steeply uphill and that made travelling the harder. Jan, leading the way, kept a very stiff pace, and Clive, who had never before been underground, began to breathe hard. He was glad when Jan paused opposite the mouth of a cross passage and held the light so as to look down it.

"Better keep straight on, hadn't we?" Chad said. "My notion is to stick to the main adit. The air's fresh, which seems to show there's an opening somewhere up this way."

"Maybe you're right," Jan agreed, "but looks to me like the roof's rotten in the adit."

"It's probably rotten everywhere," Chad said. "We've got to chance it and trust to luck."

They had gone about a hundred yards beyond the cross-cut when Jan pulled up. The light fell upon a monstrous mass of sharp edged boulders which completely blocked their way. Jan shook his head.

"Baint no passing here," he said. "Us must go back, Mr. Chad." Chad bit his lip.

"Not a hope," he said. "We must try the cross-cut. Only hope it isn't a blind alley." They turned and, reaching the cross-cut, entered it. It ran to the left—that is, to the north. Here the floor was drier and they made better time. The air, however, was not so good and the harsh odour of decay caught Clive's throat.

The cut curved slightly to the right and presently the light fell upon another block. The whole roof had given way and tons of loose rock formed a huge barrier. Jan went forward and examined the fall. Clive, just behind him, saw that the piled rocks did not quite reach the roof. There was a space a foot or so wide between the top and the gap from which the rock had fallen. It seemed to Clive that there was just room to crawl through this opening, yet the risk of doing so was appalling, for the roof was so rotten that even Clive could see that a touch would bring it down. Jan looked at Chad.

"It be bad, Mr. Chad," he said gravely.

"Let's have a look," said Chad and, taking the light, he climbed carefully up the side of the fall and looked through the gap. He came down again with equal care.

"It's clear enough beyond, so far as I can see. Shall we chance it, Jan?" Jan hesitated.

"It be taking a bad risk," he answered gravely. As he spoke there came from the distance the sound of a crash. The three looked at one another and all their faces showed that they knew what had happened. Clive spoke.

"They're after us." He set his teeth. "We've jolly well got to try it."

CHAPTER XIII

A SOUND OF STEPS

"WE'VE got to try it," Chad repeated. "I'll go first, you next, Clive, and Jan will come last."

Flat on his stomach, Chad drew himself across the great pile of jagged stones. The others stood by watching, hardly daring to breathe. Even if Clive had not seen for himself how desperate was the risk, the set look on Jan's face would have made him realize the danger. But Chad knew what he was doing, and came safely to the other side.

"Now you, Mr. Clive," said Jan, and Clive, his heart in his mouth, crawled through the narrow gap. The roof above was full of cracks and he knew that the merest touch would bring it crashing down. Then Chad's strong hands gripped him and drew him clear.

It was Jan's turn, and it seemed hardly possible that his bulky body could pass through that narrow space. He wormed forward inch by inch and Chad drew a deep breath of relief when he, too, arrived in safety.

"Put that light out," was the first thing Jan said as he gained his feet. "I want to see if those chaps be after us."

"I can hear them," Clive replied.

Someone was coming. All three could hear footsteps groping down the gallery; then after a while a gleam of light showed. Suddenly there came a savage exclamation from Jake Treslove.

"Shut up!" Ben Grint snapped. "Keep your head low like I do."

"Yours ain't as high as mine anyways," retorted Jake. "A runt like you can go where a man can't."

"I'll show you who's a man if you don't keep your mouth shut," Ben retorted fiercely. "And get on a bit quicker. We don't want to spend all night chasing these fools."

"I don't believe they're in here at all," Jake answered sulkily. "They got more sense than to climb up a fox earth like this."

"And where else would they go?" snorted Ben.

"Out through that there hole in the roof most like." Ben laughed harshly.

"And who made all them footprints in the mine? Don't be a bigger fool than you got to be, Jake Treslove. They're in the mine, and they're in this here gallery, for they couldn't be nowhere else."

Silence again, except for the sound of boot soles on rock. The light grew stronger. Then Jake spoke again.

"There! What did I tell ye? This passage is blocked just like the first one. They just made them tracks to fool you. They're a mile off across the moor this minute." Ben Grint did not answer at once. The three behind the rock fall gathered that he was a bit staggered. But his silence did not last long.

"This ain't no block. There's room atween the top o' the fall and the roof. They're over and past."

Jake laughed scornfully. "You mean to tell me a thick chap like Otter could get through that place? You're crazy."

"I means to say that's just what he have done," Ben answered.

"Be you going to follow?" Jake sneered.

"Can't do nothing else," Ben said firmly.

"Then you can go yourself," Jake answered harshly. "The money ain't minted as would tempt me to climb through there. I'd as soon put my head under a steam roller."

"And that wouldn't hurt your head," Ben snapped. He paused, and the boys realized that he and Jake were just the other side of the fall.

"See here," Ben went on in a quieter voice. "We got to catch Otter and them kids. If they gets away the whole job's blown on, and you knows what the boss will say—and do." Jake spoke:

"If you want to commit suicide I ain't stopping you. I've told you already I'm not going through that place."

"Then you know what's coming to you," said Ben ominously.

"I ain't scared," snapped Jake. "Anyhow, what's the use of money if you're dead, squashed like a mouse in a trap. Shove on and I'll go outside and I'll lay I'll have 'em afore you."

Ben went on. The boys and Jan could tell that by the sound. In a flash Jan was up with a big stone in his hands. He flung it against the roof. With a roar, tons of rock came crashing down on top of the fall. The boys sprang away and Clive switched on his torch. The air was so thick with dust that for the moment they could not see at all. When it cleared, the barrier was complete and not even a rat could have found its way through from the far side.

"What did I tell you?" came Jake's voice faintly from the other side. "You was lucky to get off alive. If you'd been a yard further, you'd have been flat as a kipper."

CHAPTER XIV

THE CHIMNEY

JAN touched his lips for silence and the three went on up the tunnel. The passage rose at a steady slope and this was encouraging. Also the floor was drier, so they got on faster. The gallery seemed endless, but Jan became more cheerful.

"Air's better," he said, and this was true. The air was certainly fresher. This seemed to argue an opening, and Chad's spirits rose. The next thing that attracted their attention was a cut in the right-hand wall. It was a sort of shaft which ran up at a tremendously steep angle. It was no larger than an old fashioned chimney.

"Air shaft," Jan said. "Reckon her goes up to top, but baint no good to us." Clive spoke:

"My torch is pretty nearly finished," he said uncomfortably. True enough, the battery was almost down and the light turning blue. Presently they had to stop and light the candle. Chad saw that there was an hour's light at most. And afterwards—well, that didn't bear thinking of, and he quickened his pace. They rounded another curve and saw something ahead. It was not a fall but the blank end of the passage. A wall of solid rock.

No one spoke. Chad was conscious of a horrid sinking feeling at the pit of his stomach. No way forward, no way back, for the rock fall had cut off any chance of return. They were hopelessly trapped, without food and with light for less than an hour. Clive's face had gone very white again; as for Jan, he stood as still as if frozen. Yet Jan was the first to recover.

"We're not done yet," he said. "There's that there shaft. Us'll have a look at un." The boys did not speak. They were afraid that their voices might betray their feelings. They turned in silence and followed Jan back to the air shaft. Jan took the candle and held it up.

"There's staples," he said, as he pointed to a great V.-shaped piece of iron fast in the rock. Chad's spirits bounded, only to fall again when he saw how terribly rusted the iron was. It was on the tip of his tongue to declare that it could never hold him, but he bit off the words as he realized that to climb this shaft was the only chance of life for him and his companions.

"I see," he said cheerfully. "I'd better go first, Jan. Then I can give you a hand." Jan hesitated a moment, then agreed. He cut the remains of the candle in two and fixed half of it in the front of Chad's hat.

"Good luck to 'ee," he said in a low voice, and Chad set forth on his perilous venture.

He gripped the first staple and drew himself up. To his great relief it held. The iron was so thick that in spite of rust there was enough to bear his weight. He stretched to the next and managed to gain it. But when he had done so he realized that it was utterly impossible for Clive, who was so much shorter than he, to climb from one staple to another. Nor could Jan do it. He stopped and looked down, and told them about it quietly.

"See here," he went on, "when I get to the top, I shall go back to the mine house for a rope. There's one there. I saw it. There's no risk, for Ben and Jake will be up on the hill, looking for us."

"Us'll wait," was all Jan said, and his quiet voice made Chad realize better than anything else the difficulty of his task. Jan would not argue, because he did not want Chad to waste breath in replying.

Chad went on. Foot by foot he won his way up that perilous place, knowing that one mistake, one slip, would mean certain death. The climb seemed endless, every muscle in his body ached, his hands were torn on the rough iron, his finger nails were split, perspiration streamed down his face, almost blinding him.

More than once he felt as if he had reached the end of his tether; it was only the thought of those others waiting beneath in the dark depths and the knowledge that their lives depended on him, which drove him onwards and upwards.

Suddenly a splash of cold rain struck his burning face and a thrill of triumph ran through his aching body. Then his candle blew out, but just above him was a dim patch of light, his groping fingers found a ledge, he gave a last desperate heave, hoisted himself over a sharp edge of rock, and collapsed flat on his face on soaking turf.

"Chad! Chad!" It was Clive's voice echoing up from the depths. Chad turned and got his face over the edge.

"I'm safe. I'm all right. Just resting a minute. It's not quite dark up here and there's plenty of cover. I'll go and have a look at the mine house. If they're there I'll go back to Badger's Holt. If not, I'll get the rope. Don't worry. I'll take no chances."

He struggled to his feet. The worst of the storm had passed, though lightning still flickered on the horizon, and it was still raining. He came upon a pool in a little hollow, stooped, drank and felt better. Crouching beside a big boulder, Chad took a look round and was surprised to find how close he was to the mine house. A flicker of sheet lightning showed it not more than three hundred yards away, but about two hundred feet below him. Feeling sure that Ben and Jake would never dream of his coming up through this shaft, he went cautiously down to the mine house.

There was no light inside, the door was not locked, he went in and found the rope without trouble. He was coiling it when he heard footsteps coming towards the door.

There was only one thing to do and Chad did it. He slipped into the inner room, crawled through the broken boards and crouched inside the mine. Next instant he heard the outer door open.

"Ben—Ben, are you there?" The voice was Jake's, but what, in the name of all that was unlucky, had brought him back?

CHAPTER XV

CHAD'S CLOSE CALL

"BEN, they're out!" Jake went on harshly. "I seed one on 'em on the hill. Come down this way, he did." There was the sound of a match being scratched, then an exclamation of surprise.

"Why, he ain't here!"

Chad didn't quite see why Ben should have been there, yet evidently Jake had expected him to be. Perhaps Ben had remained to watch the adit, in which case Jake would probably come through to the mouth in order to look for him. That thought wasn't a pleasant one, but it was too late now to do anything about it, so Chad made himself as small as he could and crouched down in the corner behind the boards. Then the inner door opened.

Chad was not easily scared, but now he was fairly shaking, for, if this long fellow spotted him, the last hope was gone for Jan and Clive. They might stay down in that black prison till they starved.

"Ben!" came Jake's voice again. He was angry now. "Drat the fellow!" he growled. "Why can't he do what he says he'll do?" He came right across to the opening and thrust his candle through.

"Ben!" he shouted once more. Chad gave up hope of escaping notice. He was on the point of springing up, knocking the candle out of Jake's hand and making a rush for it, when Jake turned away.

"He ain't here either," the man growled. "Fat-headed fool. He'll hear what I thinks of him afore he's much older."

Chad could hardly believe his senses. Somehow the man had failed to see him, and now was going back into the outer room. He was still grumbling and muttering angrily.

The question was what would the man do next, and Chad listened with quivering eagerness. He had not long to wait, for he distinctly heard Jake go out, slamming the door behind him.

Even then Chad dared not move. He waited for the longest five minutes he had ever known before he dared to creep out of his muddy hiding place, and no cat ever crossed a room more carefully than he. He peeped out of the door. The rain had nearly stopped and it was less dark than it had been. Then a flicker of lightning along the horizon showed a tall figure striding down towards the swollen brook. Chad waited no longer. Carrying the rope, he was out and off up the hill.

Afraid that the lightning might betray him, he ducked and dodged from one clump of heather to another, but saw no more either of Jake Treslove or Ben Grint, and reached the mouth of the shaft in safety. It was worth all he had gone through to hear the joy in Clive's voice as the rope went snaking down into the depths.

"You first, Clive," Chad said. "Then you and I together can haul Jan up. And hurry! Jake's somewhere down by the brook, but I haven't a notion where Ben is."

There was no great difficulty in getting Clive up, for he was a light-weight; it was a much harder job to haul up Jan's eleven stone. But somehow they did it, and Jan's gratitude was not the least of Chad's reward.

By this time, all three were so exhausted they had to rest before doing anything else, so they found a big rock and sat under it. While they got back their breath and their strength, Chad told them of his visit to the mine house, and how he had got the rope.

"Jolly good work!" asked Clive warmly.

"Baint no doubt about that," Jan added.

"Next thing is to get home," Chad said. "I wish I knew where Ben was. He's the one I'm afraid of."

"I reckon he'm gone across hill to t'other adit," Jan said thoughtfully. "Looks to me best thing us can do is to keep down into valley and follow brook. Her runs into Badger Brook."

"All right, Jan," said Chad. "You know the country, so you'd better lead. Let's push along."

They got down into the valley without seeing anything of their enemies, and went on as fast as they could. But the stream was over its banks and the bogs full of water, and the going was so bad that they were driven up the slope again. It was lucky that Jan knew the moor, for alone, the boys would have been hopelessly lost. At last Jan stopped beside a streamlet which ran swiftly down the hill.

"I reckon us have covered the worst of un," he said. "Another mile and us ought to reach Badger Brook." Clive caught Jan by the arm.

"Someone's coming," he whispered.

Jan did not waste a moment. He pointed to the deep bed of the brook.

"Get down in there," he ordered, and all three slipped over the bank and stood knee-deep in cold, swiftly running water. Next minute two figures showed up against the night sky.

"Ben and Jake," Chad whispered, as he ducked below the bank. "Don't talk. They may hear us."

For a nasty moment Chad thought they had heard, so straight did the two men come towards the place of hiding, but as Chad peered over the rim of the bank he saw that this was not the case; they were simply picking the easiest way through a lot of rough heather and rocks. As they came they were talking.

"If we don't find 'em," Jake said, "I'm going to bunk."

"Don't be a fool," Ben retorted. "What's the use of talking that way? It don't matter what they do or where they go, we're bound to get 'em."

CHAPTER XVI

WANDA'S WARNING

CHAD strained his ears for more, but the men passed on and their voices died away.

"I wish I knew where they're going and what they're after," he said. "Think it's safe to get out of this water, Jan? My feet are pretty near frozen."

Jan agreed that they might get out and, having done so, they went on slowly. The last thing they wanted was to catch up with the enemy. Not that they knew which way the others had gone. Chad wished devoutly that he did.

By this time Chad was longing for rest. He had been going hard for about sixteen hours and that climb up the shaft had taken a lot out of him. Strong as he was, he badly needed supper and bed. Clive, too, was limping.

At last they came to the Badger Brook and, though they could not see the house, knew they were within half a mile of it. Jan went more carefully than ever. The bay showed dimly in front, and, at the top of it, the bridge of the Badger Brook, but Jan would not let them go down.

"Like as not them fellows is waiting underneath," he said.

"We can't stay here all night, Jan. Let's go on quietly. If they are beneath the bridge we can be over and past before they catch us." Jan objected, but at last it was agreed that they should go down to the bridge on hands and knees, crawling among the heather.

Chad led, and had just reached the clump of gorse nearest the bridge when he almost fell over someone crouched there. He made a violent grab and heard a little cry of pain.

"You, Wanda!" he gasped in utter amazement.

"Oh, I'm so glad to see you," said Wanda in a quick, low voice. "I've been lying here ever so long, waiting for you. Those horrid men! I saw them from my window, prowling about in the garden, and somehow I felt sure they were the ones that had carried off Jan. So—so I slipped out the back way."

"It was jolly plucky of you," Chad said warmly.

"You—you wouldn't say so if you'd known how scared I was," Wanda answered. "And I was worse scared when I heard them coming straight towards the wall. I dropped down behind and simply didn't breathe. Then I heard them talking, and presently came to understand that they'd had you in some sort of prison, that you'd got away and that they were after you. They knew you had to get into the house, so they were going to wait outside till you came, then grab you."

"Where are they now?" Chad asked.

"Under the wall to the south of the house."

"Then if we go round by the north side, we can get in at the back door without their seeing us."

"That's what I was thinking," Wanda said.

"And arter that I'll have summat to say to 'em," Jan remarked grimly.

Luck was with the boys. Another heavy shower came on, and it was so dark that they, Wanda and Jan were able to walk over the bridge without a chance of being seen. Once under the north wall, they were safe from sight, and within a few minutes had reached the back door. Wanda had the key, but before she could put it in the lock the door opened and there was Rachel.

"Oh, my dear man!" cried Rachel, and, without paying the least attention to anyone else, flung her arms round Jan's neck and kissed him on both cheeks. Jan was scandalized.

"What be about, Rachel? Don't 'ee see the young gentlemen is wet to the bone?"

"We're all right, Rachel," said Chad, whereupon Rachel let Jan go and hugged him.

"It was you got Jan back for me, Mr. Chad. And you, too, Mr. Clive. I'm surely grateful." Jan cut in:

"Rachel, where be my gun? Them nasty chaps is outside this minute, and I'm bound to prison 'em." He caught sight of his old double-barrel in the corner of the kitchen, snatched it up and ran out. The boys, tired as they were, followed.

The shower had passed and it was lighter.

But when they got to the place where Ben and Jake had been hiding behind the wall, there was no sign of them.

"Scared and gone," said Clive. Jan was bitterly disappointed. He wanted to follow, but Chad persuaded him that this was foolish.

"They're half a mile away already," he said.

"But however did they know?" Jan demanded.

"Torgan warned them," said the quick-witted Clive. "His window faces the front of the house."

"Torgan. Aye, likely you're right, Mr. Clive. Us'll settle with that gent in the morning." He turned, and they went back to the house to find that Rachel had a good fire in the kitchen range and was busy cooking.

"You go right up and change," she ordered the boys. "Supper'll be ready time you comes down. You, too, Jan."

Ten minutes later, they all sat down in the kitchen to hot soup, cold beef and pickles, bread, butter and cake, and while they ate, they told Wanda and Rachel all their adventures of the past twelve hours. Wanda's pretty face grew quite pale as Chad described his climb out of the mine and his visit to the blowing house for the rope.

"So you see," Chad ended, "we were right about Torgan. There's no doubt at all that he is at the bottom of the whole business."

"But what would he want with Jan, Mr. Chad?" Rachel asked in a puzzled voice.

"To get him out of the way, Rachel. Same with us."

"Dad shall send him packing to-morrow morning," Wanda said firmly.

"He ought to go to prison," Jan declared, but Chad shook his head.

"Probably he ought, Jan, but we have no proof against him." Wanda was looking thoughtful. Now she spoke.

"I don't know how Mr. Torgan came to know of the treasure, yet it seems pretty plain that he is at the back of all this. What seems plainest of all is that he's found it." Chad's eyes widened.

"Found it!" he repeated.

"Yes," put in Clive quickly. "Wanda's right. He must have found it for, if he hadn't, what was the use of getting rid of us? Don't you see —he wanted us out of the way so that he could cart the stuff off without being disturbed."

"You're right, Clive," said Chad eagerly. "Then before Torgan goes we must have the truth from him." Jan nodded.

"Aye, us'll do that, Mr. Chad."

But disappointment was in store for all of them. When they got up next morning, Torgan had gone. He had left before daybreak in his car. In his room they found a note saying that he had been called away. All his things were gone. He had not left even an address.

CHAPTER XVII

ENEMY'S WORK

THE one person at Badger's Holt who seemed thoroughly pleased by the turn of events was Major Garnett.

"I am not surprised," he declared. "Fellow like that who fishes with a worm is capable of anything. I'm glad the man's gone. Don't suppose you'll have any more trouble now, Mr. Heriot."

"I'm not so sure," Chad said slowly. "Those two fellows, Ben and Jake, are still loose."

"What harm can they do?" asked the Major. "With you two boys, myself and John Otter, they'd have some trouble to break in—even if there is anything worth their while." He turned to his host. "I'm not talking of your plate, Mr. Heriot, but of this treasure which they're supposed to be after." Mr. Heriot shrugged.

"I believe it to be a wild-goose chase, Major Garnett. The story of plunder hidden there may be true, but, in my opinion, someone removed it long ago."

"I should say you were right," the Major answered, "but if you have any doubts on the subject it might be as well to call in the police."

"I certainly don't want the police again if it can be avoided," said Mr. Heriot. Major Garnett agreed with his host, and they went on with breakfast. Afterwards Chad, Clive and Wanda met in the garden.

"Let's try the cave to-day," Wanda said eagerly.

"Rather!" said Clive. "I'm frightfully keen to get in there and cross that pit."

"I suppose it will be all right, leaving the house?" Chad remarked.

"Why, what could happen?" Clive asked.

"I'm thinking of Ben and Jake," Chad said.

"They'd never dare come in daylight," Clive said.

"You're forgetting Major Garnett," Wanda added. "He said he'd be fishing near the house. He's trying for sea trout in the Long Pool. He thinks the flood water will have brought some up from the sea." Chad's face cleared.

"In that case we'll be all right. The only thing we shall have to watch for is that Ben and Jake don't spot us going to the cave."

"Yes, one of us will have to stay outside," said Chad with decision. "It wouldn't be any joke is they boxed us up inside the cave."

"We'd better take some sandwiches with us," Wanda said. "Then if we are boxed up in the cave, we shan't starve."

While Rachel was cutting the sandwiches, Chad had a word with Jan and told him where they were going. Then, carrying the rope and crowbar and candles, the three went off up the cliff. At the top Chad stopped and had a good look round, but saw nothing suspicious. Jan was working in the garden; the Major was fishing the Long Pool, everything seemed quiet and peaceful. Clive was in high spirits but Chad had little to say. Deep inside him he had a feeling that all was not right. If Torgan really knew about the treasure, he wasn't going to give up easily, of that Chad felt certain.

The day was fine, there was not much wind, they drove in the crowbar, fastened the rope to it, then the two boys fetched the plank which Chad and Jan had hidden in the gorse, tied it to the rope and let it down. The three went after it and reached the little platform at the cave mouth. Chad and Clive took the plank and went in.

Chad had a candle fixed in front of his hat. Jan had showed him how to do it. He lit it and they went in. The first part was easy enough, but Chad knew it would be hard work to get the plank through the narrow part. He need not have worried, for when they got to the narrow part, the passage was blocked by a pile of broken rock. Clive stared—you might say glared—at it.

"Of all the rotten luck! It's a roof fall." Chad had dropped the plank and was examining the mass of rock.

"Yes, a roof fall," he said, but in a tone that made Clive stare.

"What's up?" Clive asked sharply. "Why do you speak like that?"

"Take a look at it," said Chad dryly, "then perhaps you'll understand." Clive stood frowning, studying the fall. When he turned again, his face had changed.

"Pick marks," he said slowly.

"That's about the size of it, my lad," said Chad. "That roof didn't fall by itself."

"Then who did it?" Clive demanded. Chad shrugged.

"Torgan or Ben or Jake—or perhaps all three of 'em. We'd better get out and tell Wanda."

CHAPTER XVIII

CHAD'S BAD DREAM

WHEN Wanda heard, she looked dismayed, but recovered quickly.

"How long will it take us to get through?" she asked.

"I doubt if we can do it alone," Chad said. "In any case it will be beastly dangerous. It's a job for a professional miner."

"Jan knows mines," Wanda said. "We must fetch him."

"And leave the house unguarded?" Chad asked.

Major Garnett will be quite close. If anything went wrong, Rachel could fetch him. Besides, the cellar is locked and I've hidden the key."

"I'll go and fetch Jan," Clive offered, and Chad agreed. Wanda got Chad to take her in to see the fall. She was horrified at the great pile of broken stuff. When she came out she was very thoughtful.

"Why did they do it, Chad? Why did they block the tunnel?"

"Because they didn't want us to get in."

"Then," said Wanda, "it means that there's a way through to the cellars, or at any rate to the place where the treasure is."

"It does seem like it," Chad agreed.

They were still talking when Clive came back with Jan. Jan had a pick and shovel. He went into the cave and had a look at the fall. He shook his head.

"Going to be terrible awkward to clear all that," he said.

"It's got to be done," Chad answered, and Jan nodded.

"Us'll try. Now don't none of 'ee come too close. Us must find out if roof holds." It was wonderful to watch him as he began on the pile. He seemed to know exactly where to start and what to do. Presently he looked round.

"Roof be all right. I'll pry these rocks out one by one and you can carry them out of the way."

They set to it in earnest. Chad carried the big stones, Clive and Wanda the smaller ones. Wanda worked as hard as any of them. At last they broke through and Clive made a plunge forward, but Jan stopped him.

"Tea time," he said, "and the master'll be expecting you back. He'll be worried if you don't come. Us'll go home now and come up again after." Clive got quite angry, but Jan was firm and Wanda backed him.

"It's only waiting an hour or so," she said, "and anyhow we all want our tea—and a wash."

Clive submitted and they went out. The weather had changed again. By the time they got home it was raining so heavily that the water was running in streams down the hillside, and it was out of the question to go down the cliff in such weather. Major Garnett had come in when the rain began. He had a brace of fine sea trout, and reported that he had not seen anything suspicious all day. They told him how they had cleared the cave and he seemed quite interested.

They spent an unhappy evening. Their nerves were all on edge with the waiting and the suspense. Chad and Clive by this time were as keen as Wanda herself to find the treasure. They had both come to realize what a tremendous lot it would mean to Wanda and to her father. They tried to talk of other things, but always came back to the treasure.

The first to go up was Major Garnett. He said he was tired and wanted a good night's sleep.

"I'll lay he's not half as tired as we are," said Chad. "If he'd been shifting rocks like us he could talk."

"Most likely he'd be speechless," Clive answered with a grin. "I say, Chad, it's stopped raining."

"You'd like to start, I suppose?" said Chad sarcastically.

"I'd be game," Clive declared. Chad laughed.

"You're quite crazy. Well, we'd best turn in. We'll get off early in the morning."

They said good night and went up. The boys had two small rooms at the end of the passage on the north side of the house, then came Wanda's room, with her father opposite, and Major Garnett's was one of the two rooms facing south.

Chad was truly tired and was hardly in bed before he was asleep. He had a horrid dream. It was that he had gone down to the cellars and found a great hole in the floor. He was looking into it when someone came up behind, pushed him into it and slammed down a trap door, imprisoning him in a little dark cell where there was no air and he could not breathe.

He woke from one nightmare to another. He was actually suffocating. Something, a rug or a blanket was wrapped round his head and shoulders, a heavy weight pressed upon his body and strong hands held him down. He fought furiously, kicking and struggling with frantic energy; he tried to shout but the blanket muffled his cries and cut off his breath, while the weight on his body made it impossible to move. His struggles became more and more feeble and suddenly he collapsed.

"He'll do now," came a gruff whisper. "Is all clear outside?"

"All clear."

"Then help me down with him."

It is pretty bad to be choked till you are insensible, but it is almost worse coming to again. For one thing it takes so much longer. Chad found himself choking and coughing and struggling desperately to get air back into his starved lungs.

He was trying, too, to sit up, but this he could not do, for his hands were tied fast and so were his ankles.

As his head cleared, he began to realize that the place he lay in was pitch dark and that he was lying on cold stone. His head throbbed horribly, his throat was equally painful.

By degrees the shock began to pass, his lungs worked again and blood flowed through the choked veins of his body. Memory came back and with it recollection of how his nightmare had changed to horrible reality. He groaned in misery, and the groan brought an echo—but it was not an echo. It was another groan. He realized suddenly that he was not alone in his prison. He had a companion hidden in the blackness.

CHAPTER XIX

JAN LOSES HEART

"WHO'S there?" Chad asked, hoarsely.

"It be Jan, Mr. Chad. So they got you, too," he added bitterly.

"They got me all right," Chad said. "I woke with a blanket over my head. I don't know what happened after that. When I came to, I was here. Where are we?"

"I don't rightly know," Jan answered, "but I knows who put me here. It were that Torgan."

"Torgan! But he left—ran away."

"Her did that just to put us off scent, so to speak." Chad tried to collect his scattered wits.

"But how did he get into the house?"

"That's what surely beats me, Mr. Chad. Yet he were in all right."

"You saw him?"

"Be sure I saw him. It were this way, Mr. Chad. Yesterday morning, afore I went up to the cave, I fixed two boards in the passage by the cellar door so they'd creak if anyone trod on them. It were not Torgan I were thinking of, but them two chaps, Ben and Jake. I hadn't been in bed an hour when I heard the creak, and up I got. I slipped on a pair of trousers and my old rubber soled shoes and went down. Didn't have no light even. Sure enough, there were Torgan."

"But how did you know if you had no light?" Chad asked.

"Her had one. Her were just opening the cellar door. Had a key all right."

"One he'd made himself, I suppose."

"Not a doubt. If I'd had sense I'd ha' come back for you, but I were so afraid of missing him and so sure as I could tackle him myself, that I only waited till he were inside the cellar afore I went after him.

There he was with his torch, stooping over a flagstone in the floor. He did something—I couldn't see what. Part of the wall swung back just like that door Miss Wanda found into the secret cellar—only this were in the left hand wall. Then Torgan stood up, went right across and walked through the opening.

I gave him plenty of time afore I followed. I were a bit excited, for I reckoned he'd found the way down to this here Plunder Pit, as Miss Wanda called it, but I went quiet as a mouse, and I could see his light a bobbing along a good bit ahead. The passage were cut in solid rock, and good as the day her were made."

"Didn't you have a stick or anything?" Chad asked.

"Aye, I had kitchen poker," said Jan and went on: "Passage curved and his light went out of my sight round the curve, but I could still see the glow of it. What I didn't see was that the floor were wet with drip from the roof. Next thing I knowed I were slipping. Couldn't hold my feet nohow, and come down with a crack that nigh scatted my brains.

Before I could get my senses again the fellow were on me. His hands be like iron. I never knowed he were that strong. He nigh choked me afore he let go. Then he turned the light on me.

"'I thought it were you, Otter,' he said, speaking quiet as you like, but there were a glitter in his eyes as fair scared me. Then he rolled me over, put his knees in the small of my back and tied my wrists with a length o' cord. He jerked me to my feet and dragged me along. I couldn't say how far we come, for I were fair dazed with the tumble and the scragging he give me. All I know is we come out in a wide place and there he dumped me down, tied my ankles and went back up the slope. A few minutes later he come by again and went on past me."

"Then the odds are we are actually quite close to the Plunder Pit," Chad said. He lowered his voice to a whisper. "Got a knife, Jan?"

"No, Mr. Chad, and if I had I couldn't reach un."

"I know, but I thought I might."

"Baint no way of getting loose, far as I can see," said Jan bitterly. "And meantime that nasty thief'll get away with all the stuff, whatever there be."

"Our only hope is if Major Garnett should come after us," Chad answered.

"Bain't likely. Her sleeps like dead."

"Then Clive will get in from the cave."

"Like as not, Mr. Clive be trapped like you and me," said Jan.

"They haven't brought him here anyhow," Chad answered. Jan did not answer and Chad lay still, thinking hard. Presently he spoke again.

"I can't imagine how Torgan got into the house. The doors were bolted as well as locked, so false keys wouldn't help him."

"Broke a window, most like," Jan suggested. "That Jake were a proper burglar." Chad spoke again:

"The fact that they came in through the cellar seems to show that they mean to go out again the same way. In that case, Torgan will have to come past us again."

"Won't be no use asking him to let us loose," Jan said. "Her be hard as this rock we're lying on."

"Hush!" Chad told him quickly. "Listen! What's going on?" From somewhere in the distance came a sharp snapping sound which echoed dimly down the dark rock passage.

CHAPTER XX

WANDA WAKES

WANDA ought to have slept as soundly as Chad, yet when she got into bed she could only doze. She kept on thinking of all that had happened and wondering what they would find in the cave next morning.

Again and again she tried to put it all out of her mind and get to sleep, but it was no use.

The rain had quite stopped, there was no wind. If it had not been so quiet, the odds are that Wanda would never have heard the very faint sound of a door near by being opened. Wanda sat up and listened hard. Presently she heard something else. The boards in the passage creaked as though under a heavy weight.

Wanda slipped out of bed. She turned the handle and got a horrid shock when she found that the door would not open. The key was inside, so it was not locked, but she could not move it. She examined the door and found that it was fixed by means of a wooden wedge jammed under it from outside.

"Wanda's hobby was chip-carving. She drew the blinds, lit a candle, found a mallet and chisel and, muffling the chisel with a handkerchief, managed to push the wedge out. She put on a dressing gown over her pyjamas and peeped out. All seemed quiet.

She stole across to Chad's room and knocked twice. No answer, so she opened the door and went in. The room was empty, the bed was all in confusion, the clothes pulled off on to the floor. Chad's slippers lay by the bedside, his dressing gown hung on a peg.

If Wanda had been frightened before, now she was terrified, for it was clear to her that something had happened to Chad. She was so panic-stricken she could hardly think what best to do. But that did not last long. She pulled herself together and went straight to Clive's room.

The first thing she saw was that his door, too, was wedged just as hers had been. She did not waste a moment in snatching out the wedge and went straight in.

"Clive!" she said urgently. Clive was sound asleep. She shook him awake.

"Clive, Chad's gone. Someone's taken him away. Get up—quick!"

Clive came out of bed like a rocket. He thrust his feet into slippers and rushed into Chad's room. One look was enough for Clive.

"It's Jake and Ben. They've got in somehow." He snatched the candle and went down the stairs, flying. Wanda followed. There was no sign of anyone about, and the house was silent as a grave. The first thing Clive did was to try the cellar door. It was locked, but as he turned away he stopped short.

"Look at those marks," he said, pointing to footmarks on the floor. "Mud," he added, "and hardly dry yet. Someone's been in from outside." He went swiftly to the front door. "Hulloa!" he said sharply. "The bolts are drawn."

"They were closed when I came up," Wanda answered.

"Someone's been in this way," Clive said. "Yes, look at the marks. Big feet. Jake's, I'm pretty sure. Wanda, I'm going out to see. You wait here."

There was light enough for Clive to find his way down the drive and just outside the gate he caught a glimpse of some dark mass. It was a car with the lights out. He crept up and cautiously examined it. The car was a Buick, and Clive recognized it at once. Then he hurried back to the house.

"Torgan's car is at the gate," he told Wanda. She stared.

"Torgan! But he went away."

"Just a blind. He's back and I expect he has Ben and Jake with him. They've collared Chad of course, but I'm hanged if I know where they've taken him. Wanda, we must get Jan and Major Garnett."

"I'll go for Jan," Wanda said quickly. "You wake up Major Garnett." She ran upstairs and Clive followed. A couple of minutes later they met again on the landing.

"Jan's gone," Wanda whispered, "and Rachel doesn't know where."

"Garnett's gone, too," Clive told her.

Wanda's lip quivered. This was too much, and for a moment she could not even speak. Clive took charge.

"Wanda, they must be in the cellar. Those chaps wouldn't have bothered to break in here like this and collar Chad and Jan unless they had to get something out of the cellar."

"But there's nothing there," Wanda argued.

"There must be," Clive insisted. "They've found something which you don't know about. Where's the key?" Wanda ran to the kitchen and got the key out of a drawer. She put it into the lock and turned it. Then she tried the door. It would not open. Clive tried but could not move it.

"Fastened from inside," he said; "probably wedged just as your bedroom door was. Wanda, this makes it a flat certainty that they're down there somewhere." Wanda bit her lip.

"Oh, Clive, what can we do? There's no one to help."

"There's you and me," said Clive stoutly, "and Rachel. See here, Wanda, what about screwing up this cellar door? Then they can't get out, and after that the best thing we can do is to go round to the cave and get in that way. The plank is there and the passage is open. If we can find Jan and Chad and Major Garnett and turn them loose, we ought to be able to settle those three robbers."

CHAPTER XXI

VOICES FROM THE PIT

RACHEL stood by them in dressing gown and slippers. She had heard Clive's suggestion.

"I'll get candles and things," was all she said. Clive and Wanda fled upstairs and in almost no time were down again fully dressed. Clive had taken thought to bring Chad's slippers. He also had a knife.

Rachel had an old-fashioned candle lantern. It wouldn't blow out, she explained. Besides, they could cover the light, if need be, with a cap or handkerchief.

"And I'll fasten the cellar door. Be sure of that," were her last words as the two slipped out.

It was lighter than it had been. The clouds were breaking and stars showing through. At the gate Clive stopped.

"I'm going to put that car out of commission," he told Wanda. He opened the door, got in and took off the brake. The car stood on a slope and at once began to move. Clive steered her to the side of the road and ran her into the ditch.

"One thing—whatever happens, they won't get away with the plunder," he remarked with satisfaction. Then he and Wanda turned up the steep slope. The short summer night was drawing towards dawn as they reached the top. Clive was relieved, because going down that hillside in the dark would be no joke. The rope was where they had left it some ten hours earlier, fastened firmly to the crowbar. Clive went down first and Wanda followed.

Clive went into the mouth of the cave, struck a match and lit the lantern. Then he walked slowly forward, picking his way among the boulders which littered the floor. He and Wanda crept cautiously through the cleared space and both drew deep breaths of relief when they saw the plank still in position, just as they had left it. They crossed it and paused on the far side of the rift.

"Wonder if we ought to leave it there," Clive said.

"I don't think we'd better meddle with it," Wanda answered. "We might not be able to get it back if we wanted it in a hurry."

"Dare say you're right," Clive agreed, and was moving on when Wanda stopped him.

"Better put something over that light. We don't want to be spotted by anyone down below there." Clive put a handkerchief over the lantern and again they went on cautiously. The passage was more open and there was plenty of head room.

"Looks as if it had been cleared at some time," Clive whispered. Wanda caught his arm.

"Listen!" she said. A voice came up to them, muffled by distance yet perfectly clear.

"Keep your hands out of that! You hear me?" Clive stopped as if shot.

"It—it's Torgan," he muttered.

"It's Torgan," Wanda repeated. "Oh, Clive, we're right. He is down there."

"Yes, and who else?" growled Clive. As if in answer, a second voice came to them. A voice so harsh and ugly it made Wanda shiver.

"What's the matter? I ain't doing no harm."

"And you won't while I'm watching you," retorted Torgan, and his tone was filled with a ferocity which made even the other man's seem mild.

"It's Jake," Clive told Wanda. "Jake is with Torgan. They must have found the plunder and are quarrelling over it. We're in pretty company, Wanda."

Wanda did not reply at once. She was listening hard. From this spot she and Clive could hear but not see, so it seemed plain that the passage in which they stood led down to the chamber where the treasure was hidden, but that it curved so as to cut off all sight of the Pit. There was not even any reflection of the light which the thieves must be using.

"They're packing the stuff," Clive said.

"And Jake's trying to help himself to some of it," Wanda added. "What are we going to do?" she went on. "You and I can't tackle two big men."

"There's only one thing to do so far as I can see," Clive told her. "Clear out." Wanda stared.

"Clear out? Run away and leave those wicked thieves to steal everything? You're joking, Clive."

"Not a bit," Clive answered. "If we go back up the passage and take the plank away they are prisoners. The cellar door is fastened. Rachel has seen to that. And your father will be there with his shot gun. Rachel will have told him. They can't get the stuff out or get out themselves." Wanda shook her head.

"That's true enough so far as it goes, Clive, but you are forgetting Chad. They have Chad and Jan down there and Major Garnett, too, I expect. Just think what they may do to them if they find themselves trapped."

"Yes," said Clive slowly, "they can hold them and use them to make terms." He shook his head. "We're certainly up against it, Wanda."

CHAPTER XXII

CHAD, THE SCAPEGOAT

A CLANKING sound came from below, then a panting as of someone carrying a heavy weight.

"That's enough," came Jake's unpleasant voice. "I can't carry no more."

"Right. I can take the rest." The speaker was Torgan. "And that'll be the lot."

"Good job, too," said Jake sulkily. "And don't forget we've got to take it through the house. And the woman's there, and the old man, too."

"You attend to your own business," retorted Torgan. "I'll see to that." There came a growl from Jake, but no words that Clive or Wanda could hear. Wanda turned to Clive.

"Now's our chance," she said quickly. "They're going back into the cellar with the plate. If we slip down into the treasure place we can let Chad and Jan loose."

"You're right," said Clive. "Only don't say 'we.' This is my job."

"No, Clive. I must come, too."

"You're not coming, Wanda. Your job is to go back to the gap. Cross it, and be ready to pull the plank away. It's on the cards that Grint may be there and chase us. It'll make all the difference if someone's ready there to pull the plank away the moment we're over."

"I suppose you're right," said Wanda.

"I know I'm right. I'm going now. You take the lantern. I have the flash."

"Clive, you—you'll be careful," begged Wanda.

"Be a fool if I wasn't," replied Clive as he started. Wanda watched till the tiny thread of light from his torch was lost round the curve, then turned and went quickly back up the passage.

Clive moved down the slope as quickly as he dared. Seeing a sharp curve in front, he switched off his light, and that was just as well because next moment he saw a glow in the distance. He also heard a shuffling of feet as of men carrying heavy loads. Torgan and Jake, he felt sure, though he could not see them.

He paused a moment, then, since he could neither see nor hear anything else, went on again.

Presently he realized that the passage was widening. He paused again and listened hard. He could still hear footsteps, but the light was gone and the blackness in front unbroken. This was a relief, for it meant that none of Torgan's men had been left behind.

The sound of steps died away, but still Clive listened. He longed to switch on his light, but did not dare to do so. Then another sound came to his straining ears. It was someone breathing —breathing quickly as if excited. This person,

Clive realized, was not far off. Clive decided to risk it.

"Chad!" he whispered.

A moment's pause; then Chad's voice in a joyful whisper.

"You, Clive! I knew you'd come. I told Jan."

"Jan there, too? I say, Chad, is it safe to switch on my light?"

"You'll have to. We're tied neck and crop. I think it's all right. Torgan and Jake have gone up to the cellar."

"Where's Ben?"

"Don't know. Haven't seen him. Quick, old lad. Cut us loose."

Clive hesitated no longer. He switched on the torch, and swinging its tiny beam across the rock floor, saw Chad flat on his back, bare-footed, clad in nothing but his thin pyjamas. Jan in shirt and trousers lay beside him. There was blood on Jan's face. Clive came across like a shot.

"Are you hurt, Jan?" he whispered.

"Took a fall. Baint nothing to speak of. Cut Mr. Chad loose." Clive had his knife ready. He slashed away the cords round Chad's wrists and ankles and Chad was on his feet in a moment.

"Here are your slippers," Clive said, as he pulled them out of his pocket.

"You're a brick," said Chad with warm approval. "Hurry up with Jan. We have to get clear before those robbers come back."

"They'll come back all right," Clive said.

"Rachel has wedged the cellar door and Mr. Heriot is in the passage outside with his shot gun."

"Good man!" said Chad. "You got in by the cave, I take it."

"Wanda and I," Clive answered as he cut Jan loose. "Wanda's waiting up by the gap. If we bunk out that way and pull the plank after us we have them boxed beautifully."

"We'll have to hurry," Chad said. "We want to get back to the house and give the others a hand. Jake has an axe, and they'll tackle that cellar door for a certainty. They won't give up the treasure very easily."

"They've got it, then?"

"Every bit of it. Took 'em four journeys to carry it up to the cellar. It was all in that big chest there." He pointed as he spoke to a huge, old wooden chest standing against the wall of the cave.

Jan was loose. Clive tried to help him up, but Jan fell down again.

"It be my head," he said hoarsely. "That fall. Give me a minute and I'll be better." The two boys looked at one another in dismay. Both knew that they had not a moment to waste. They ought to be running back for the gap as hard as they could go.

"We'd better each take an arm and help him along," said Chad in a low voice. Before Clive could answer there came another voice, Torgan's, and though distant it came down the rock passage as if through a speaking tube.

"The door's fast. The woman must have locked it."

"I told you we'd ought to have attended to her afore we started," Jake snapped back. Torgan said something that was certainly not a blessing. His voice sounded savage as that of a trapped wolf. Then the boys heard him roar:

"Open that door. Open it quick, whoever's the other side." If there was any answer the boys could not hear it. Then Torgan spoke again to Jake.

"Go back into the cellar and fetch the prisoners. When they hear what we're doing to them I'll lay they'll open the door quick enough." Clive spoke swiftly:

"Come on Chad. We have to get Jan out of this." Jan made a struggle to walk, but was so giddy he staggered and would have fallen if the boys had not caught and held him. Clive felt almost desperate. To have done so much, and all for nothing, was simply heart-breaking.

"Take hold of him. We must carry him," he said fiercely.

"Can't be done," returned Chad. Then suddenly his face changed. "I've got it," he went on swiftly. "You and Jan hide behind that chest. I'll stand here and wait for Jake. When he sees me, I'll bolt. I can outrun him."

"But he might shoot."

"He won't. He wants me alive, not dead. Give me your torch, and get behind the chest, quick as ever you can. Here, I'll give a hand."

There was no time to argue, for already they could hear Jake coming down the passage, so Clive helped Chad to steer Jan in behind the chest. There was just room between the chest and the wall for the two to crawl in, but, once there, they were completely hidden. The moment they were safe, Chad leaped away and ran noiselessly on slippered feet to the upper mouth of the Treasure Cave. He had Clive's torch, but as he reached the spot from which he meant to make his start, he switched it out. Next moment Jake's light lit up the end of the opposite tunnel and the great gaunt figure of the man showed in its gleam.

Chad was in a tight place and knew it, yet, in spite of this fact and of the deadly danger, the sight of Jake's face, when he saw that his prisoners had vanished, nearly made him laugh. The man's jaw fell, his eyes bulged. He stood staring at the spot where Chad and Jan had been lying as if he could not believe his senses. Then suddenly he came to himself.

"They're gone," he roared. "Torgan, they're gone."

CHAPTER XXIII

THE THIRD MAN

"GONE !" came Torgan's voice, echoing down from th e black depths of the tunnel. "You're crazy. They can't be gone."

"Come and see for yourself, if ye don't believe me," yelled back Jake.

Chad heard Torgan's rubber-shod feet thudding down the rock passage and realized that it was time to move. He flashed his torch full in Jake's astonished face and sprang out into the open.

"Not gone, but going," he jeered as he turned and raced up the tunnel.

With a howl of fury Jake launched himself after. But the only light he had was a candle stuck in his hat and, of course, the draught caused by his rush promptly put it out. Chad did not see what had happened, but Jake's yell of rage told him that something was wrong.

The noise Jake made brought Torgan tearing to the rescue.

"What's up?" he thundered.

"That there Chad. He and the other have gone up that passage. He stopped to give Otter a chance to get away."

"And you let him go!" Torgan's raging voice reached Chad's ears and made him run faster than ever. Which was just as well, for Torgan had a flash and, snapping it on, did not waste an instant in starting the chase. He could run, too, and his legs were longer than Chad's.

So long as he lives Chad is not likely to forget that wild race up the rocky corridor. He had never been along it before, for he had not crossed the gap the previous afternoon, and he had not had time to ask Clive about it. He was terrified of coming to a low place and banging his head against the roof. If he were caught, that finished everything. Torgan would drag him back, Torgan would find Clive and Jan and, with three hostages, would certainly be able to dictate terms to poor Mr. Heriot. For another thing, Chad did not know how soon he might reach the gap, and at the pace he was travelling there would be no stopping if the plank was not handy. He had to take the chances, for, by the sound, it seemed to him that Torgan was gaining. The man was desperate and would strain every nerve to catch him.

Where was that rift? Chad's flesh crawled at the thought of plunging into those black depths. He remembered the length of time that had elapsed before the splash came back, after he had dropped the stone.

Suddenly he saw a faint glow ahead and his heart leaped, for he knew this must be Wanda's light and that she was keeping faithful watch over the bridge. The light grew stronger, he saw Wanda's slim figure holding up the lantern. Its gleam fell upon the yellow surface of the plank. With one stride he reached the middle, with a second he was across and, flinging himself down flat on his face, he seized the plank and jerked it back.

Torgan must have seen it being dragged away, but he was coming too fast to stop. He made a wild leap, his head struck the low roof with a sickening crash, and he fell flat on his face on the far side, stunned and insensible.

"Get back, Wanda!" Chad said swiftly for, by the sound, Jake was coming hard behind.

"Stop, you idiot!" he yelled to Jake, but Jake had no idea of stopping. By the light of Wanda's lantern he could see her and Chad plainly, but he either failed to see Torgan or did not realize what had happened to him. With a howl of fury he came on full pelt.

At the last moment he saw the great black gap and jumped. He, too, struck his head heavily against the rock roof and his luck was not as good as Torgan's. Before Chad could catch him he had dropped into the depths of the chasm. There was a sullen splash, then silence. Wanda went as white as paper.

"Is—is he dead?" she gasped.

"Jake is. Don't worry, dear. Now we must get Clive and Jan. And—and the treasure."

"Not yet," came a harsh voice, and out of the

darkness behind him a man sprang on Chad and flung him down, falling on top of him. The unexpected attack, the force of the fall, almost knocked the senses out of Chad, but he was not really hurt and, after the first surprise, began to struggle furiously. So furiously that his opponent had his work cut out to hold him. For his age Chad's strength was amazing and, arching his body, he actually lifted the other clean off the ground; but, do what he would, he could not loosen the man's grip The floor sloped to the edge of the chasm, the two rolled over towards it and Chad realized that in another moment they would both be over.

The other saw it, too, he shifted his grip, got one arm around Chad's neck and began to force his head back.

The pain was dreadful; Chad's strength was leaving him; he was almost helpless when there came the thud of a blow, the light went out and all was plunged in utter darkness. But at the same time his enemy's grip relaxed and his body went limp. With a last effort Chad rolled free and lay panting, too done to move.

"Chad! Chad!" came Wanda's voice.

"I'm all right," Chad answered hoarsely. "W-what happened?"

"I hit him with the lantern. I had to."

"I should jolly well think you did. He was fairly scragging me. You did fine, old girl. What about a light?"

"I have matches. Don't move, Chad. You're dreadfully near the edge." Wanda's hands shook so that she had a job to light a match.

"The lantern's broken," she said.

"There are plenty of candles," Chad said cheerily, as, by the light of the match, he got up and drew away from the edge of the gap. "And here's our enemy's torch," he said, as he picked it up and switched it on. It flashed at once and Chad, stooping, turned over the limp body of his latest opponent. A gasp of utter amazement came from his lips.

"It's—it's Garnett," he said in a tone of flat unbelief.

CHAPTER XXIV

TIDYING UP

GARNETT it was—there was no doubt about that, but the shock of the discovery left the two almost speechless. Wanda was the first to recover.

"This explains a lot," she said. "Now we know how Jan was got out of the house and Jake let in. Chad," she added angrily, "he's worse than Torgan."

It was at this moment that Chad noticed signs of Garnett returning to life. At once he was his practical self. Spotting a silk handkerchief sticking out of Garnett's pocket, he took it, rolled him over on his face again and tied his wrists firmly. With a second handkerchief he made his ankles fast. He had just finished when Garnett's eyes opened and he tried to move.

"I'd keep still if I were you," Chad said curtly. "You're pretty near the edge." He left him and set to work to make Torgan safe. He was still insensible.

"Now for Clive and Jan, Wanda," he said as he pushed the plank back into position.

"You're not leaving me here in the dark," said Garnett.

"We certainly are," Chad told him. "Keep quite still and you'll be all right. If you move you'll save the police a lot of trouble." Another minute and he and Wanda were on their way down to the Plunder Pit.

"You got them both!" exclaimed Clive, when he heard what had happened.

"All three," Chad told him. "Garnett's one of the gang."

"Didn't nohow like that man," said Jan, who by this time was recovering from his fall.

"It's a rum business," Clive added thoughtfully, "but you and Wanda have done fine, Chad." He paused. "Better get back to the house, hadn't we? There'll be a lot of ends to tidy up."

"A lot," Chad agreed. "Come on."

Wanda led the way with the light. Chad and Clive, one on each side of Jan, helped him along. The secret door was now wide open and the first thing they saw when they reached the cellar was a number of sacks bulging with tarnished plate.

"All old stuff," said Clive, who knew something about plate. "That silver is pretty well worth its weight in gold."

"Oh, boys, and you've done it all," said Wanda with a little choke in her throat. Then she raised her voice. "Dad, it's Wanda and the boys and Jan. We're all right. You can let us through."

After a little delay, the door at the top of the steps opened, and poor Mr. Heriot went quite white when he saw the battered procession emerge. Rachel grabbed Jan and hugged him.

"My poor old man," she said. "You come along up and I'll soon put you right." Then to the others: "The kitchen fire's burning and there's water boiling. Make them some tea, Miss Wanda. I'll be down soon."

Over cups of hot and welcome tea Mr. Heriot heard the story of the last hour.

"Garnett in this, too!" he exclaimed. "It's hard to believe that any Army man could belong to such a pack. But one thing is certain, I'll never have any more paying guests," he declared with unusual energy.

"You won't need to, sir," Chad assured him. "The treasure is safe in the cellar and you and Wanda will be rich."

"Let's go and see it," Clive suggested, but Chad shook his head.

"Plenty of time for that. What we have to do is to fetch the police and give those three fellows into custody."

"And I hope Sergeant Eve will be grateful," said Wanda tossing her head.

"Well, you have done what he couldn't do," Mr. Heriot said quite briskly. "The next question is how are you going to get to Bulport. It is unfortunate that we have no telephone."

"We'll use Torgan's car, sir," Clive told him. "I shoved it into the ditch to prevent his using it, but we'll get the old pony and soon have it out."

"That's the ticket," said Chad. "Just wait till I get some clothes on. I can drive a car, and I dare say they won't make a row even if I am too young to have a licence."

By this time it was broad daylight. While Chad changed, Clive and Wanda led the pony out of the stable and put harness on it. They got plough chains and fastened them to the back axle and Chad came out, fully dressed, just as they had all ready. Wanda held the pony's bridle and made it pull while the boys shoved, and in a minute or two the car was up on the road again. It was decided that Wanda should go with Chad, and Clive stay at home to look after the house in case anything went wrong; then Chad started the car and he and Wanda drove off.

It was still so early that they met no traffic, and Bulport was only just beginning to wake up when they got there. They drove straight to the police station and here a bit of luck awaited them. Sergeant Eve was in bed with a chill and the man in charge was a big, kindly constable named Buxter. His eyes fairly bulged when he heard the story that Chad and Wanda had to tell, but he wasted no time in collecting a second man, and very soon Chad was heading back for Badger's Holt. Not a word was said about Chad being too young to hold a driver's licence. Indeed, the policemen were so interested they probably never gave the matter a thought, and all the way Buxter was asking Wanda question after question about the recent events. Wanda answered them as well as she could, but Chad chuckled inwardly to hear how little she said about the treasure.

As they came up to the house, they were relieved to see Clive waving to them from the front. Chad had been wondering all the time if Ben Grint might not have turned up and made trouble. But there had been no sign of him, and the minute the car stopped, the police got out and Buxter began to talk to Mr. Heriot. Clive drew Chad aside.

"I've covered up the plate sacks," he told him. "No need for the police to see more of 'em than need be."

"Good man!" said Chad. Then Mr. Heriot called him, and he and Clive took the police down through the cellar, and on through the passage to the place where the prisoners had been left. Buxter handcuffed Torgan and Garnett and took them out. The others sighed with relief as they saw the car with the prisoners drive away; then Rachel called them all to breakfast.

It was the cheeriest meal since their arrival, and the cheeriest of the lot was Mr. Heriot, who seemed to have grown ten years younger since the dread of losing his beloved home had been lifted.

"The only trouble is that I'm afraid the State will take at least half of the treasure," he said. But Clive reassured him.

"Dad's a barrister," he said, "so I know a little about that sort of thing. The plate isn't Treasure Trove because it belonged to your ancestor. I expect they'll make you pay inheritance duty, but that's all."

"I shan't grudge that," said Mr. Heriot with a sigh of relief. "The thing I would suggest is that you boys have a share of it."

"Of course," cried Wanda. But Chad waved a hand.

"Nothing doing, sir. Thanks to our people we're all right. We'll take our share out in fishing for your trout. We haven't had a chance at them yet."

"You shall have all the trout in the river if you can catch them," Mr. Heriot promised. "And you can take your time about it, for you can't leave yet. You'll be needed to give evidence—remember."

"Splendid!" cried Wanda. "I hadn't thought of that. Then you'll stay the rest of your holiday?"

Clive chuckled.

"You couldn't drive us away, eh, Chad?"

"I'll stay as long as you'll let me," Chad answered frankly. "It's the nicest place I ever stayed in—and the nicest people. Now let's go and inspect the treasure."

PRINTED FOR THE PUBLISHERS BY
PURNELL AND SONS, LTD. PAULTON (SOMERSET) AND LONDON

Oh, for a booke and a shadie nooke,
Eyther in-a-dorre or out;
With the grene leaves whisp'ring overhede,
Or the streete cryes all about.
Where I maie reade all at my ease,
Both of the newe and olde;
For a jollie goode booke whereon to looke
Is better to me than golde.

Old Rhyme.

Publications of
FREDERICK WARNE & CO. LTD., LONDON & NEW YORK

MAJOR CHARLES GILSON

THE TWELFTH MAN

Incorrigibly cheeky and daring, yet sportsmen every inch, are Buttenshaw and Slade Two. They are as enterprising and entertaining a pair of schoolboys as could be imagined. Their feud against the unpleasant master, Roach, is rollicking fun. But there is an earnest side to this book, that of the cricket pitch. The breathless thrill of a closely fought game is described with a vim that holds the reader to the last page.

(*Published in the Albion Library*)

TABOO

Into the heart of dark Africa with "Cinderface", the reliable, reckless and never-despairing explorer. Across burning sand deserts and through terrifying jungles, seeking the country of the Urrjard where malignant evil broods over the Place of Death. Packed with tense moments, startling adventures and vivid descriptions, this story is neither exaggerated in detail nor improbable in incident.

(*Published in the Magnet Library*)

THE SUBSTITUTES

Cricketers, and all interested in our great summer game will enjoy this book. It is a school story with cricket as the main motive of life. There is a village cricket match, where cricket is played in the traditional style of the village green, and there is a grimly-contested inter-school match. The connection between the two makes a very interesting story.

(*Published in the Magnet Library*)

HYLTON CLEAVER

THE TERM OF THRILLS

Two public schools in one town, and a twin in each school! Eric and Stanley are indistinguishable, and keep their twinship a secret. Complications, comic and grim, occur when the twins secretly visit each other's school. Credit and blame are heaped on the wrong head, and their exciting and amusing struggles in the meshes of muddle, make thrilling reading. Every page is enjoyable.

(*Published in the Albion Library*)

BUTTLE BUTTS IN

Buttle was not strong in character or muscle, and was easily led into trouble. He wanted to go back to his old school, and went—as a kind of "gate-crasher"; but those who were in the secret were determined to get some fun out of the novel situation, and poor Buttle was forced into a series of scrapes. An exciting and humorous story.

(*Published in the Treasure Library*)

THE PHANTOM PEN

Exciting mysteries! The unknown hand that penned the evil letters! The fist that could batter bully Trumble! The parts played by the elusive Jackson and the "Rat"! The inimitable, dry and elaborate Mr. Mott! Adventure! Cass versus Hegarty in the ring! Plot and counterplot! Full of humour, and a bona fide school story that keeps the reader intent from beginning to end.

(*Published in the Treasure Library*)

GURNEY SLADE

THE DELTA PATROL

"The World's most plausible rogue" was the description of Othman Bey, given by Eddie of the Delta Squadron, Australian Imperial Forces. Certainly his cunning trickery made Victor's holiday in Egypt a venturesome affair. The author of "In Lawrence's Bodyguard" more than maintains his excellent reputation for story-writing in this tale.

(*Published in the Albion Library*)

LED BY LAWRENCE

The Turks were great fighters, but the Bedouin had a fiery energy that only needed organising and unifying. This was the task of Lawrence, whose name is for ever linked to Arabia in our Empire history.

Jasper—young, strong and daring—meets and works for Lawrence; and his adventures in the Secret Service make a story the more thrilling for being based upon amazing fact.

(*Published in the Albion Library*)

T. H. SCOTT

THE TREASURE TRAIL

A motor launch of marvellous speed is constructed by Sam. He and Bill meet Jake, the adventurer, who has a chart of a golden treasure in the City of the Sun, in the Amazon basin. They decide to seek the gold, but strange happenings are theirs before they reach the Evil Land.

(*Published in the Globe Adventure Library*)

A. L. HAYDON

THE SKIPPER OF THE TEAM

Aylmer or Venables? The School was divided in its allegiance. Aylmer was not only a fine footballer and scholar, but a genius at acting. In disguise he could deceive his own schoolmates, except the acute Challis—and the crafty little Cowl. A yarn of school life with really "live" characters.

(*Published in the Albion Library*)

KIDNAPPED FROM DOWNWAYS

Cheng Fu, the mysterious Chinese, dominates the story. He kidnaps Roy from his school, suddenly and secretly, then takes him by air and sea to China, where exciting adventures follow one upon the other.

(*Published in the Magnet Library*)

POLE FOR COCK HOUSE

A first-class school story. Old house feuds and meddlesome juniors make trouble. Through all this discord strides Coke, the new school captain, a budding poet yet a stalwart of the rugger field. Steadily he forges his way into supreme popularity, and wins honour for his house. Games and sports are vividly described, particularly the great boxing match.

(*Published in the Magnet Library*)

ADMIRAL SIR E. R. G. R. EVANS, K.C.B., D.S.O., LL.D.

THE EXILE

Noel Howard, son of Admiral Sir John Howard, had to flee the country because of the plotting of his rascally Russian cousin, Ivan Shermann, who faked a strong charge of murder against him. Even then Ivan's hatred was not satisfied, and he pursued his cousin through France, Belgium, Russia, and at last to Norway, where Noel had his final reckoning. The long exile over, Noel was able to return to his Devon home, in time to join Nelson's navy, preparing for the last tussle with the French. A finely-written and unusual story by one who loves and understands the sea.

(*Published in the Treasure Library*)

NOEL HOWARD, MIDSHIPMAN

In this thrilling story of the sea, Noel Howard, the red-haired, snub-nosed Devon lad, becomes a Midshipman in the Navy, in the days when Nelson was hurling his ships against the French. Fights with French frigates and men-of-war, cutting out expeditions, adventures in the Spanish Main, and finally, in escaping from his French captors, a journey across unknown Africa, make up a stirring tale. But it is something more than a tale of adventure ; it is an authentic picture of the life in the Navy in the hazardous days of sail ; and through it runs what the Author calls " the clear fresh call of the sea."

(*Published in the All Time Library*)

E. KEBLE CHATTERTON

ACROSS THE SEVEN SEAS

Racing across the Atlantic, through Panama, out into the Pacific in a fifteen-ton yacht—surely Paul and Rodney were fortunate in having Commander Marshton, R.N., for an uncle! But it was not all plain sailing. The international crook, Hjort, did his utmost to ram and wreck the little craft. A splendid tale of the sea.

(*Published in the Magnet Library*)

IN GREAT WATERS

Chinese pirates of modern days! Chang Kling's mighty submarine roves the seas from Shanghai to Plymouth, destroying and pillaging. On the trail of this ruthless and cruel sea-thief is a tiny craft, fitted only with a small quick-firer, and manned by Captain Harwood, V.C., and the two boys, Bob and Wilmer. The great game of hide-and-seek played by these two foes makes a yarn rare in plot and real in atmosphere.

(*Published in the Magnet Library*)

THROUGH SEA AND SKY

The super-flying boat "Gannet" is commissioned to track down the mysterious "Black Rovers" who have stolen the formula of a terrible Z ray from Admiralty Room 909. Captain Harwood, Bob and Wilmer speed through the air at nearly three hundred miles per hour, fighting the great red aeroplane. Altogether a yarn that sets the pulse beating high with the spirit of courageous venture.

(*Published in the Magnet Library*)

CAPT. F. A. M. WEBSTER

THE BOY FROM THE BLUE

Living in wild Africa until sixteen, strong and supple as forged steel, Jim Dawson comes home to public school life. His first efforts at rugger, in the boxing ring and classroom are vigorous and amusing. But his father falls among rogues in Africa, and Jim goes back to the rescue. A yarn of stirring adventure.

(*Published in the Albion Library*)

HYLTON CLEAVER

CAPTAINS OF DUKE'S

Cricket, boxing and rugger Captains—each with his own problems and difficulties. The descriptions of matches in each sport are exciting and real. Never to be forgotten is the schoolboy detective who, with Holmes-like flair, elucidates mysteries by original and ingenious schemes.
An entertaining and brilliantly written book.

(*Published in the Magnet Library*)

T. C. BRIDGES

THE RIVER RIDERS

Keith Hedley, on the way to his uncle's lumber camp, is set upon by two rough and tough villains. He wins through to the camp, but there he comes against the brute bully Hulke Hansen and cunning old "Granite." The thrilling drive when chased by a pack of grey timber wolves and the adventure on the flooded river are outstanding in a tale full of breathless, stirring incidents in wildest Canada.

(*Published in the Albion Library*)